Dancing Alone

"It's my life, Doug. I can't stop dancing."

He reached warm hands across the table and laid them over mine. "Honey, honey," he said, "I never asked you to stop dancing. Only to dance in Boston instead of San Francisco."

I looked across the table at him, at his pale smooth lips that I had kissed so many times. My insides dissolved.

"That's why I had to come tonight, Mag," he went on, "to ask you to marry me and come to Boston."

I pulled my hands from beneath his. I shook my head. "I can't. I just can't. I have to dance here. Ballet companies are hard to get into. I've got a start here. People know me. One choreographer's even giving me a role in a new ballet he's doing this summer."

"Trouble is, Mag, you don't love me enough!"

Other Avon Books by
Karen Strickler Dean

BETWEEN DANCES: MAGGIE ADAMS'
EIGHTEENTH SUMMER

MAGGIE ADAMS, DANCER

Stay On Your Toes, Maggie Adams!

Karen Strickler Dean

AN AVON  FLARE BOOK

AVON BOOKS
A division of
The Hearst Corporation
1790 Broadway
New York, New York 10019

ACKNOWLEDGMENT

My thanks to members of the Parents Alliance for the Mentally Ill of Santa Clara County (California), an affiliate of the National Alliance for the Mentally Ill, 1200 15th Street, Suite 400, Washington, D.C., 20005.

Chapter One

Five important events took place on my nineteenth birthday. The first happened outside the dressing room as I rushed to ballet class. In my cubbyhole on the lowest tier of company mailboxes slanted a thick yellow envelope.

Snatching it, I glanced at the address, then stared. Look at that handwriting! Capitals reared like horses. Halos dotted the *i*'s. Crescents slashed the *t*'s. My heart somersaulted. A letter from Doug. The address began:

Ms. Maggie Adams, Apprentice Prima Ballerina
City Ballet Company (or some such name)
Geary and Fifteenth Avenue (or somewhere thereabouts)
San Francisco, California 94130

I pressed the envelope to my chest. Tears stung my eyes. I could almost hear him humming as he addressed it. Humming, smoothing his beard, and smiling. Smiling at his joke. Which happens to be mostly true. I am with City Ballet. I do live in San Francisco. I do dream of becoming a prima ballerina although now I'm only an apprentice.

I sighed and pushed at a friz of red hair that came sliding out of my topknot. Receiving the apprenticeship was why I changed my mind about moving to Massachusetts with Doug last August. That hot, sultry morning was the only time I ever saw him cry. Tears glistened along the lower rims of his eyes and on his pale, thick lashes. Then he ducked into his orange sports car and careened away

1

from my house. Brake lights winked as he took the corner. His horn beeped, then nothing. Nothing! Not a word in nearly ten months until this letter.

I slid a finger beneath the flap of the envelope.

"Whatever it is, Mag, you don't have time to read it now," called my roommate Joyce from behind the reception desk.

She pointed at the foyer clock. Five minutes past eleven. The class for company members and apprentices begins at eleven. Whispering, "Oh, please say you're coming back, Doug," I pushed his letter unopened into my satchel and took the stairs three at a time. In the studio I dropped my bag on the pile of satchels near the door. Thank heavens, class hadn't started yet!

I searched the large high-ceilinged room for a place to work. The *barres* teemed with dancers dressed as I was. Washed-out pink tights, ash-gray leotards faded from black, stretched leg warmers, tattered sweaters knotted at the waist.

Only Natalie Harper, our prima ballerina, warming up at a choice location directly opposite the wall of mirrors, looked the way a dancer is supposed to look. A low-cut black tunic bared her snowy back and hugged breasts no bigger than mine. Her black hair clung to her small neat head. Its blue sheen paled her oval face to ivory. The elegant poise of her body and head left no doubt that she was a ballerina. She might have been taking a curtain call and presenting her partner with a flower from her own bouquet. Even from here by the door, her mysterious musky perfume overwhelmed the piny scent of rosin, the stink of sweat, and the bland sweetness of my own Johnson's baby powder.

I sighed, feeling like a gawky kid. I mean, I'm taller and slightly heavier than Natalie. Also, I have this frizzy red hair and a spattering of freckles left over from when I actually was a kid.

"Maggie, there's a place at the portable *barre* near the back," called our teacher, Eleanora Martina.

I scurried to the opening. It was right behind Kathy, my other roommate and a brand-new apprentice.

"Guess what, Kathy?" I whispered. "I got a letter from Doug!"

"That gorgeous man you went with in high school? Wow! Is he coming back?" Before I could answer, Martina clapped her hands, signaling class to begin. I lowered my knees to the slow rhythm of a Chopin étude our pianist always uses for *pliés*.

My body, legs, and arms moved easily in exercise after exercise. During a *rond de jambe en l'air* combination, Martina stopped beside me at the *barre*. She gave me her beautiful smile.

"Your left foot is arching nicely in the *relevés* this morning, Maggie."

Glowing, I stretched taller to arch it even more. It's my weaker foot, the one whose ankle I've sprained a couple of times.

After we moved to the center of the room I balanced the *adagio* variations without a wobble. But in the mirror I glimpsed Natalie Harper's *arabesques* flowing into *attitudes*. Would mine ever look that exquisite?

"Nice high extensions, Maggie!" Martina said. I pushed my working leg even higher.

"No sense overdoing it!" Martina said before turning her attention to other dancers.

But for me the best part of any class comes near the end with the jumping combinations. Today one included *grands jetés* and *tours jetés*.

"Dance full-out," Martina said. "Travel around the room. Faster dancers pass on the outside. Divide yourselves into four groups. First group starts."

She motioned me to join the first group, which, as usual, consisted of the company's top soloists and principal dancers. Including Natalie Harper! I gulped. I mean, I'm still only an apprentice! Martina must have noticed my hesitation to join this elite group. "It's so every group has an equal number of people, Maggie," she explained.

"Wow!" Kathy whispered beside me. "Wish I could

jump like you! Me, I'm the original lead-foot! With these dumb feet of mine I wonder if ballet and I are made for each other. But you!'' she added, giggling, ''that *ballon* of yours is really getting you up there! In more ways than one!''

I ignored her silly pun because just then the great Natalie Harper was taking the starting position for the combination directly in front of me. Really nervous, I pushed at a wisp of hair and crossed my fingers, somehow sensing that today's second important event was about to happen.

When the music began, I soared around and around the room in one stretched-out leap after another. Soon it wasn't only my muscles lifting me. It was also that wonderful exhilaration that dancing sometimes brings. I call it my summer wind.

I must have circled the studio a dozen times, passing dancer after dancer, including Natalie Harper. Suddenly, right behind me, a shriek, then a thud. The music halted. I landed from a *grand jeté*. On the floor in front of the mirror sprawled the ballerina. I peered down at her. What should I do? My face grew hot.

''Gosh, are you hurt, Miss Harper?''

She didn't answer. Just moaned, rubbed her ankle, and rocked over it, forward and back, forward and back. Thank heavens, here came Martina with a cluster of dancers.

''What happened, Natalie?'' Martina asked.

''My tendon. My tendon,'' Natalie Harper wailed.

I poked at my hair and chewed my lip.

''I hope its not ruptured, Miss Harper,'' I said, frowning. I mean, a ruptured Achilles tendon, in spite of the latest surgical techniques, usually ends a dancer's career.

''It is not ruptured, thank you, Maggie Adams,'' she snapped in that harsh, shrill voice of hers, which is so inconsistent with her beauty. ''But it could have been ruptured, the way you were chasing around the room like a circus pony. You could have maimed me!''

''What?'' I cried, tears raining down my cheeks. ''Oh, I'm sorry. I'm sorry. I really didn't touch you, though. You must have tripped.''

4

But Natalie Harper kept on screaming. "You cut right in front of me. Oh, the pain! The excruciating pain!" Skin strained at the sides of her mouth, sagged along her jaw, made her look her age. At least thirty-five.

"Will somebody please get me an ice pack or help me out of this place or do something?"

It was Armando, a fellow apprentice last year and now a new company member, who scooped her up in his arms. She clamped her pale hands behind his dark, muscular neck. She beamed into his face. "Why, thank you, darling," she said as he carried her into the corridor.

Class ended fifteen minutes later with me still really upset about Natalie. I was groping inside my satchel for Doug's letter, praying that it said he was coming back, when the day's third important event began.

"Maggie, Larry Randall wants to see you in his office right away," Martina called.

I sighed. Almost sobbed. "You know how he hates me, Madame. Has ever since I was fourteen. Remember when you both came down to guest-star in *The Nutcracker* our little company put on?"

She smiled. "Yes. The time my tendonitis kept me from dancing." Then she added, laughing, "I've always thought that the real reason Larry refused to let you replace me was that he believed partnering a kid who still wore braces on her teeth would damage the superstar image he was trying to build even five years ago."

I twisted a friz of my hair. "He was pretty awful, all right, and was only *premier danseur* then. Now he's that, plus having Bob Morris's old job. Temporarily, I hope. What really worries me is that Randall has already signed every one of last year's apprentices into the company except me, the only girl. Do you think it's my contract he wants to see me about now, Madame?"

"I'm sure it is, Maggie. And better not keep him waiting. Since Bob resigned, Larry's crankier than ever. Together fifteen years, then, instead of taking Larry along with him to Southwest Ballet, as everybody expected, Bob up and left him. It's as if my own husband, after marrying

5

me in my teens, suddenly left me to take a job in, let's say, Texas. But Larry's temper will improve, no doubt, if and when the Search Committee makes his temporary appointment permanent.''

I shuddered. ''Don't even think that, Madame!''

Shouldering my ballet satchel, I hurried out of the studio, down the stairs, and across the foyer. The brass plate on the red-lacquered door still read ROBERT MORRIS, ARTISTIC DIRECTOR. Please, God, that it would never read LARRY RANDALL, ARTISTIC DIRECTOR!

When I opened the door, Larry Randall was sitting behind Bob's gleaming oak desk. The only thing on it was a manila folder with my name on the upper right-hand corner. I caught my breath and crossed my fingers.

Eyeing me, Randall swung back and forth in a swivel chair that needed oiling. His nostrils contracted, then expanded. They do when he's angry. And he usually is.

''I believe it's customary to knock before entering,'' he drawled. He still speaks with a Western twang although he left home, some hick town in Idaho, nearly twenty years ago to study ballet first in Salt Lake City, then in San Francisco. He'd been only sixteen.

With most people his remark would have been a mild rebuff, even a joke. Not with Larry Randall. He wasn't smiling. He fixed me with ice-blue eyes that bulge like marbles.

''Take a load off your feet, Ms. Adams,'' he said, going from stilted speech to Western slang. ''There's a chair by the door. This'll only take a jiffy.''

Randall glanced at papers in the manila folder. At the same time he raked his yellow hair with a big-toothed comb, which left furrows in his pompadour. His yellow T-shirt was stamped across the chest in three gradually enlarging tiers of green letters, the top row small, the bottom enormous: Larry Randall, LARRY RANDALL, L A R R Y R A N D A L L. He tilted his head to show off his movie-star profile.

''In her report your teacher claims your technique has become cleaner and stronger,'' he said. ''But you've been

6

her prize pupil ever since you came here, so she's got to be biased.''

"Why, she's the most impartial," I began, feeling my face flame.

"Please, Ms. Adams, don't butt in!''

His long fingers scratched through more sheets of yellow paper the same shade as Doug's letter. I sighed. Oh, Doug, please say you're coming back! In a classroom upstairs a piano tinkled. Feet scraped, thudded, and thumped.

"Here's the school's evaluation of your work during the past year," Randall said, fanning more yellow sheets at me. "The consensus is that you worked fairly hard, have nice *ballon*, good elevation, and are a quick study. There is mention of your taking over a lead at the last moment in *Les Sylphides*, but, of course, it was only a studio matinee.''

Randall shuffled pages again. "Before he left, Bob Morris turned in a report that makes nothing crystal-clear but, as usual, waxes highfalutin. Bob says, 'There is a lovely youthful charm in Maggie's interpretations.' Then this bombast: 'Sometimes she tends to be overly athletic, but no doubt maturity will metamorphose Maggie from athlete to artist.' Hogwash! But then Bob always was a pushover for nymphets like you. Keyryst!'' he added, grinding the word between his teeth and glaring at me, "just this morning I found out he up and married that two-bit soloist he promoted to ballerina when he took over Southwest Ballet.''

I pushed at my hair and chewed my lower lip. It wasn't my fault Bob Morris got married!

Randall shifted more papers and squawked his chair. "Now to get to the nitty-gritty, Ms. Adams. There are reports here about your sassing a wardrobe mistress and—''

"What?'' I sputtered. "When?''

"Silence, please. As I was saying, sassing a wardrobe mistress, talking back to a stage manager, and walking out of a rehearsal, saying your ankle hurt.''

"Well, it did!'' I cried.

"And just this morning, I'm told, while having the gall to work with a group of principals, you were responsible for Natalie Harper falling and straining her Achilles tendon.''

''I wasn't. I was not!''

''So it seems, Ms. Adams, that you still have a lot of maturing to do, in your behavior as well as in your dancing.'' His words twanged like flat violin strings someone is plucking. ''But since I've always been one to encourage young dancers, I'm not chucking you out entirely as perhaps I should. Instead I'm renewing your apprenticeship for a second year.''

''A second year!'' I saw Randall's face through a furious red tide. ''You can't do that!''

''Temper! Temper!'' he said. ''Consider a moment, Ms. Adams. I may not be offering you the lead in *The Nutcracker*, but under the circumstances, a second-year apprenticeship is not to be sneezed at!''

I jumped up. I tried to keep my voice steady. ''Okay, Mr. Randall. All right! I—I have no choice. But someday I will dance the lead in *The Nutcracker!* Just see if I don't!''

Pivoting, I charged out of his office and straight into the arms of a slender, wiry man. Blikk Eriksen, the famous Norwegian choreographer!

''Oh, I'm sorry,'' I said. ''So sorry. Are you hurt? I just seem to be running into everybody today! Oh, please forgive me!''

Then, backing away, I dashed across the foyer, past the refrigerator full of Tabs and ice packs, past the company mailboxes, and into the dressing room. There I collapsed. I mean, bumping into Blikk Eriksen was the absolute end! And the fourth important event that took place on my nineteenth birthday.

Chapter Two

Most of the dancers had changed clothes and gone when I rushed into the dressing room. Only Kathy remained. She was bent over double, rubbing a knobby, bruised foot.

"Good grief, Maggie, now what's happened?"

I shook my head and sagged onto the bench. I dropped my satchel on the floor.

"It can't be that bad," Kathy said.

"It is. It is," I said, and gradually spilled the whole story of my awful morning. I omitted only the part about Natalie Harper because Kathy had witnessed that.

"Well, not getting a contract is pretty bad," she said, "but finally, a year late, I got an apprenticeship, so, if my dumb feet hold out, we'll be apprentices together. And as for running into Blikk Eriksen, I should have that kind of luck! I hear he's just back from the Caribbean after getting a quickie divorce. So he's available, and if you weren't still hung up on gorgeous Doug . . . ."

"Well, I am," I said. "Guess I'll always be. And he is gorgeous. But, gosh, I haven't read his letter yet. Maybe he says he's coming back."

I ripped open the envelope. Not a letter at all. Some kind of crazy birthday card. A knock-kneed ostrich teetering on stubby *pointe* shoes. Inside, a printed message: "I remembered. Never say I'm not on my toes! *Don't* Stay on yours. Happy Birthday." Then his scrawl, "Doug."

He had inked in the *Don't* himself. Tears rose in my

9

eyes. The same stupid put-down about my dancing! So nothing—not a thing—had changed!

"Just forget him!" I said. "How can he—how can he be so juvenile!"

I crushed the card in my fist. But maybe there was a note on the back. I flipped the card over. Nothing. Not a line about his first year at MIT after transferring from UC, Berkeley. Not a word about what he was doing this summer. So who cared? Just exactly who cared?

I ripped the card in two, threw the halves in the wastebasket, then drooped against the cold wall. Tears that had been collecting all morning flooded down my cheeks.

Frowning down at me, Kathy shifted her feet.

"Well, uh, Maggie, if you're going to make like a fountain all afternoon, I'll go pick us up a couple of yogurts. Or are you going back to the apartment?"

I shook my head to both questions. The thought of food knotted my stomach. And I didn't have enough strength to walk the two blocks to our place.

"Well, then, if the sun's finally out, I guess I'll walk over and eat in Golden Gate Park," Kathy said. "Spend the entire afternoon there. After all, it's our last free afternoon. Rehearsals begin tomorrow."

Sighing, I reached into my satchel for a tissue. Rehearsals for a summer season when I would still be an apprentice. Always an apprentice, never a company member. Sort of like being always a bridesmaid, never a bride. Oh, Doug!

"Maybe I'll run into Armando at the park," Kathy was saying. "Unless he's still holding Natalie's hand! Did you notice how he just couldn't wait to pick her up this morning? She's practically old enough to be his mother, for gosh sakes!"

Which wasn't true, unless Natalie had had him when she was fourteen. Armando's twenty-one, exactly Doug's age. Armando used to go with Kathy before switching to Anita, a member of the *corps de ballet*.

"Wish me luck in the park," Kathy said, and padded out of the dressing room in huge, run-over-at-the-heels

10

running shoes. They made her thin ankles look even thinner. Then, before the door could close behind her, she returned, huffing as if she had just completed sixty-four *fouettés*. She brushed back her pale, straggly hair.

"He's out there again, Maggie!"

"Who? Armando?"

"Don't I wish! No, Blikk Eriksen. What incredibly sweet gray eyes he has! He asked me to ask you to come out and talk to him."

"Me?" I said, bolting upright. "Are you sure he meant me?"

"He said Maggie Adams, the girl with the lovely red hair," she added, grinning.

I swallowed. "What can he want?"

"How should I know? You're the one who ran into him," Kathy said, smirking. "Anyway, better get out there before he changes his mind. Shall I tell him you're coming?"

I nodded, and while she shuffled out in her big shoes, I ran to the sink and cranked on the ancient faucet. I ducked my face into the gush of cold water, wet the end of my towel, and dabbed it under my arms. I sure wished I had brought along something to wear other than these blue jeans and this gray sweatshirt. I gave my frizzy hair a couple of strokes with a brush, then raced into the foyer. I mean, I longed for Doug but didn't intend to become a nun, for gosh sakes. He was the one who left me.

"Looking for somebody, Mag?" my roommate Joyce called from the reception desk.

I shrugged. "Not really."

I saw her wry half smile and heard her low, throaty laugh.

"Blikk Eriksen's over there, if you're looking for him."

"How did you know?" I asked quickly.

"Give me a break, doll. This is wise old Joyce. Friend from McMichael's Ballet School down the peninsula. Besides, through my trusty new contacts I saw you collide with Eriksen outside Randall's office."

I groaned.

"Also, I heard him ask Kathy to find you," Joyce added. "He's over on the sofa near what now, unfortunately, is Randall's office."

I spotted Blikk Eriksen, but he wasn't alone. Above him on the arm of the sofa perched Natalie Harper. She was smiling into his face, fanning her lashes, tilting her neat, dark head, wriggling her spidery, white fingers.

"Let him know you're here, Mag," Joyce said behind me, her round face beaming above her round body. She quit dancing and enrolled at U.C. Berkeley after finding out that she was too stacked and sturdy for ballet, as she puts it. She graduated in English, which, according to my father, prepares you for absolutely nothing, and took this job as receptionist. She wanted to be near ballet, where her talents lie in creating rather than performing. She won a certificate for choreography at a regional conference five years ago and just last summer an honorable mention in a choreographic competition held right here.

"Do your really think I should interrupt Blikk Eriksen now?" I asked Joyce. "I mean, he and Natalie look pretty cozy. Besides, she claims I maimed her this morning."

"Forget Natalie, Mag. He sent for you, didn't he?"

I edged to within a few feet of the beautiful couple. She in an elegant white wool challis dress and high heels, in spite of the ice pack tied around her left ankle. He in a white turtleneck shirt and crisply pressed gray slacks.

"Uh, excuse me, Mr. Eriksen. Did you want to see me?"

Natalie Harper's eyebrows flew up.

"You again, darling?" she asked.

Blikk Eriksen smiled and sprang lightly to his feet.

"Ah, here you are, young lady. If you will excuse me now, Natalie, we will continue this conversation later."

Then, gazing at me, his "sweet gray eyes," as Kathy called them, turned silvery.

"How lucky we collided this morning, you on your way out, I on my way into that fellow Randall's office," he said, speaking with a slight Norwegian accent. His sentences tilted a little at the ends, as if he were always asking

12

questions. His vowels came from his throat. That must be because he grew up in Norway before leaving to study and work in England and Germany. "Your name is Maggie Adams."

I wasn't sure whether he was asking or telling me.

"How come you know my name?" I blurted, then blushed because I had blurted.

"I had the pleasure of seeing you dance *Les Sylphides* when I was in San Francisco briefly last month. Such a blithe, innocent little sylph you were too. Let me introduce myself. Blikk Eriksen."

I gazed at him wide-eyed.

"As if I didn't know," I said, beaming. "As if anybody even slightly connected with ballet wouldn't know," I added, blushing but unable to stop gushing. "There are articles about you everywhere these days, Mr. Eriksen. Last month *Ballet News* claimed that you are the most brilliant choreographer to come from a German company since Stuttgart's John Cranko."

"They exaggerate just a little," he said, still smiling, his eyes silvery and crinkling.

"Oh, no. And at only thirty-three, they said."

He laughed. "Thirty-four. They are off by one year. But even thirty-three must seem ancient to you, Miss Adams."

"Oh, no," I said again, then, realizing that he was teasing me, I must have turned scarlet. Not only did I keep repeating myself, I also was practically grunting out monosyllables while he was expressing himself in perfect—really courtly—English.

And I couldn't stop staring at him. You only have to look at Blikk to know he's a dancer. His straight back. The lift of his head. The quick, almost birdlike way he moves. He is lean, wiry. Not much taller than I but so masculine. I mean, a man doesn't have to loom six-feet-four like Doug to be manly! Gray threads weave through Blikk's light brown hair but don't make him look old. Oh, not at all. Only more distinguished.

13

It was his gray eyes, though, turning silvery again, that caught at my heart. A delicious shiver danced through me.

"Gosh, what are you doing here at City Ballet headquarters, Mr. Eriksen?"

He grinned. "Well, let me see. This morning I had the pleasure of quite literally running into a beautiful young redhead."

I blushed again. "I'm sorry I was such a klutz!"

"No need to apologize. I have been wanting to meet you ever since seeing you in *Les Sylphides*."

He glanced at the slim, efficient-looking digital watch on his wrist. I noticed the branching tendons on the backs of his hand. His wrist bone stood out like a marble. My fingertips trembled to touch the hard, smooth knob.

"I see that it is lunchtime, Miss Adams," Blikk Eriksen said. "Maybe we could talk over a sandwich or a bowl of soup. Unless, of course, you are one of those American dancers who subsist on diet sodas and yogurt."

"Oh, no," I said quickly.

"Oh, no, what?" he asked, smiling. "Are you refusing my invitation? Or denying that you starve yourself?"

My face blazed. Usually I can carry on fairly intelligent conversations. I always did with Doug, even the times we quarreled about those statuesque girls he used to go out with when ballet took up too much of my time. At least, I think I did. But with Blikk Eriksen everything I said came out wrong.

"I just mean that I'm not on a diet," I said, my face burning clear up to my eyebrows. "In fact, I brought a sandwich from home today."

Which was a lie. I hate sandwiches. Besides, we almost never keep sandwich makings in the apartment. Kathy and I diet, and while Joyce may not be a dancer anymore, she at least talks about watching her weight. "If I get much fatter," she says, "I'll look like a hippo beside sylphs like you and Kathy."

"Save your sandwich, Miss Adams," Blikk Eriksen said. "I have a conference all afternoon so would like to use the lunch hour to talk with you. Please say yes."

I wriggled my shoulders and sort of giggled. "Well, okay. Thanks a lot."

"Come along, then, but first I must confer with the receptionist."

"With Joyce?" I asked, wide-eyed.

"Yes, with Joyce Mallory. I want to confirm my afternoon appointment. I will join you in a moment."

Waiting for him beside the double glass doors, I saw their heads almost touch over the appointment book and their fingers slide together down a page. Joyce's throaty laugh rolled across the foyer. I bit my lip. But why should I feel jealous of Joyce? She's my roommate and best friend. Besides, she was not the person going to lunch with Blikk Eriksen. I was.

Chapter Three

"Miss Mallory recommended a small French restaurant called La Fleur Bleu. Is that all right?" Blikk Eriksen asked me after he finished talking to Joyce.

"Anywhere," I said, but pushed at my hair. For some reason Joyce suggesting a restaurant for what I thought of as my first date with Blikk Eriksen cast a tiny shadow over my excitement. Or was it this particular restaurant?

"I imagine that you go there quite often since it is nearby," he said as we walked down the street.

Naturally I do. It's only around the corner from my apartment and just a few blocks from Ballet Headquarters. Doug and I ate there sometimes while he was a student at U.C. Berkeley. A sudden memory of him humming and studying the tall menu brought the sting of tears to my eyes.

"No. Oh, no, I've never been here before, Mr. Eriksen," I said as we turned onto the concrete apron in front of the restaurant. Now, what made me lie?

"Good," he said. "And since the sun is finally breaking through the fog, shall we eat outside?" He held a wrought-iron chair for me, then sat down opposite. He smiled across two yellow rosebuds in a tiny carafe. Lemony sunlight glinted off the glass and off the white tablecloth. His silvery eyes glinted at me.

"How nice that, although I am a stranger to San Francisco, I have the pleasure of introducing a native to a restaurant in her own city."

"What?" I flushed, then remembered I had lied about having been to La Fleur Bleu before. "I'm not really a San Francisco native," I said quickly. "I was born and grew up about forty miles down the peninsula from here. My parents still live there. And I'm wondering, Mr. Eriksen," I added, fidgeting with a spoon, "I feel awfully uncomfortable having you call me Miss Adams all the time. Please call me Maggie."

There came that smile again and the silvery look.

"I would certainly hate to have you feeling uncomfortable, Maggie. And you must call me Blikk."

"Oh, well, that's different. You're so famous and all."

He went on smiling. "How old are you, Maggie?"

"Well, nineteen," I said, blushing and wondering why he asked. I mean, that was a question people ask children, not grown women.

"Hmm," Blikk said, and two faint lines creased the pale skin above his long, thin nose. "Not that it matters, but last night Randall said you were eighteen."

I caught my breath. Why had they been talking about me? "I was eighteen yesterday," I said. "Today I'm nineteen."

His smile showed two rows of small, even teeth. Had he worn braces when he was a kid in Norway like I did here?

"Then I have the honor of taking you to lunch on your birthday, is that correct? Are you having a happy one?"

"Oh, yes!" Then, biting my lip, I remembered Doug's awful birthday card, the second-year apprenticeship, and my run-ins with Randall and Natalie. "Now I am," I said, lifting my head and shaking back my flowing hair.

"Good."

He smiled at me across his folded hands. How white they were. How neat his blunt, square nails. How unlike his hands mine were with my blotchy orange freckles and the three ragged nails I broke off yesterday, trying to pull the shanks out of some old *pointe* shoes. I curled my hands into fists and sank them into my lap under the snowy napkin.

Blikk picked up the long, narrow menu.

"Will you let me order for you, Maggie? Or are you one of those beautiful but independent American women who insists on choosing for herself?"

I flushed. I mean, I knew he was teasing me. Any answer I gave would sound silly.

"Ah, but my question is unfairly phrased," he said. "There is no question about your being beautiful. The only question is whether you will allow me to order for you."

"Oh, yes," I said, and melted against the back of my chair. I let my head spin pleasantly in the sunlight and took a deep breath of the sharp salt air. Here I sat, about to have lunch with gorgeous Blikk Eriksen!

That was when I noticed the waiter who winks and calls me "carrot top" every time I come here. He was advancing toward us, order pad in hand. Dear God, he'd be sure to betray my lie about never eating here before.

Sure enough, he smirked, winked, and said, "It's been a while, carrot top."

I wanted to disappear.

Blikk drummed his fingers on the tabletop. "We wish to order immediately," he snapped, then did so in rapid French.

The waiter stiffened and jerked back his shoulders. Poising pencil on pad, he craned around Blikk to see the menu.

"Excuse me, sir, could you show me where it says that?" he mumbled respectfully. No more winks or smirks out of him!

"*Mais oui*," Blikk said. He repeated the order in French while pointing to where each item appeared on the menu. If it hadn't been for my own awful embarrassment, I might have enjoyed the waiter's.

After the man left Blikk raised his eyebrows. "I am afraid his French is a bit rusty, but then, he is not European, is he? I consider it rude of waiters to be familiar with patrons." Then, laughing a little, Blikk added, "No matter how many times the patron has been to that restaurant."

I blushed furiously. "I don't know what made me lie."

18

"Maybe you have painful memories of this place."

I shook my head. "No. Well, some." Biting my lip, I stared at the gleam of sunlight on my napkin. Since reading that awful birthday card from Doug, I'd felt so hollow, as if all my insides had been scooped out. I mean, I'd really, really lost him! "Once—once we had a quarrel here," I told Blikk, "the guy I used to go with and I."

I frowned at the shimmering tablecloth. My throat clogged up. I couldn't recall exactly what the fight was about. I only remembered plunging out, then looking back to see Doug ducking his head to avoid hitting the frame of the door our waiter was now retreating through.

"Sorry, Maggie. If I had known . . ." Blikk began.

"No. No," I said, wagging my head. "No! Everything—absolutely everything is over between Doug and me. I—I know that now. It's just that around you, I feel so—so gawky."

He threw back his head and laughed. "Gawky? No, Maggie, a better word is *innocent*. Which is what you are. A shining American innocent. And that is why I want you in a ballet I am creating."

"Really, Mr. Eriksen? You're doing a ballet for us?"

"Yes. I came to San Francisco for that reason. I will be setting several ballets on your company during the coming year, including one I shall call *The Volcanoes*. It will preview at the studio during the summer, then be restaged for the spring season at the theatre."

An excitement as dazzling as the June sunlight filled me. I drew a deep breath. Well, even if Doug was gone, Blikk would be here a long, long time!

"For a while," he continued, "I did not think that fellow Randall would let me have you in the cast. He is doing a ballet, too, I understand, and must have wanted you in it."

"Not me!"

Blikk's eyebrows rose. "No? If that is true, I am glad. Last night we had it out, and he finally agreed I could have you."

"Last night?" I asked, my voice quavering. "Just last night?"

"Why, yes, Maggie! Last night after I returned from the Caribbean I had dinner with Randall and some of the staff. But I see I have upset you. Would you rather be in Randall's ballet?"

I shook my head. "Oh, no, it's not that. I'll love working with you."

"Then why the tears in your lovely green eyes?"

"Because—because I just realized that the only reason Randall didn't kick me out of the company entirely, kept me here as an apprentice, is because you asked to have me in your ballet."

Blikk handed me an immaculate handkerchief. I dabbed it at my eyes. "Oh, I'm sorry. So sorry," I said.

"Please cry if you like, Maggie. As I used to tell my dancers in Europe, my shoulder is always available. Whenever they needed me, I was there to help."

I had finished crying by the time the now subdued waiter set a delicate potato omelet in front of me. I didn't recognize the herbs that flavored it.

At home Mama, especially after starting college a few years ago, never bothers with fancy seasonings. I found I was really hungry and gobbled down every bite of the egg concoction.

"You see?" Blikk said, then added a sentence that could be either question or statement. "That was better than slimy, cold yogurt."

My face burned. So all the time he knew I had also been lying when I denied that I diet.

Later he insisted on ordering chocolate mousse and fragrant coffee for us. He drank his black. Usually I do, too, but today I poured enough thick cream into my cup to turn the coffee a buttery tan. It was my birthday, after all.

Now came the check and the awkward part. Stupid Doug used to get mad when I wanted to go Dutch. Suddenly it came to me, along with the prickle of more tears: That was what we had been quarreling about here! I yanked my wallet out of my jeans just as I had then.

"How much is mine?" I demanded to know.

"Ah, but this is my treat, Maggie," Blikk said gently. "Today is your birthday. These are for you too." He fished both yellow rosebuds out of the flask and handed them, dripping, to me.

I pressed them to my nose. My heart caught. A snide birthday card from Doug but lovely, sun-colored roses from Blikk! I'd keep them for ever and ever. Amen.

After he paid the check Blikk said, "Shall we walk back together? Or were you going somewhere else?"

"Oh, no," I said. I had really planned to head straight to our apartment, then phone Joyce to bring home my satchel. Instead I went with Blikk. A shiver spun through me when he took my arm. First lunch. Then roses. Now, walking along together, arm in arm. No wonder I felt as light as the thin streamers of fog flying overhead. Forget Doug!

Back at the studio Blikk hurried off to his appointment, and I, for some reason, not wanting even to look at Joyce, ducked into the dressing room. A big mistake, because there sprawled Kathy with her bluish-white, bandaged feet propped on her ballet bag.

"About time, Maggie! So how was lunch with Mr. Ballet?"

"All right. Okay," I said, hiding the yellow rosebuds behind my back. "Nothing special. Just business." I pulled my satchel from under the bench and started for the door.

"What do you mean 'business'?" Kathy asked, leering at me. She pulled on a pair of dirty white socks, then eased her tender, swollen feet back into the enormous dilapidated running shoes she wears for comfort.

"Oh, you know. Where I studied ballet. How many years. Things like that. And how was your lunch in the park?" I asked, mainly to take her mind away from Blikk Eriksen.

She hunched her skinny shoulders. "Lonely. I saw Armando heading south with Anita on the back of his Yamaha. Do you think he could have been taking her home to Sunnyvale to meet his mom?" she asked, sighing.

21

I shrugged, glad to have taken Kathy's mind off Blikk, but that night in our apartment, she started in about him again.

"So did you meet him after you dashed out this afternoon, Maggie?" she asked during a commercial at the beginning of a M* A* S* H* rerun.

"Who are you talking about?" I asked.

"Blikk Eriksen, of course! The one who gave you the roses," she said, snickering. She stretched a skinny, bare foot across our orange-crate coffee table and, with a long, fat, bandaged toe, nudged the jelly glass holding my two yellow buds.

Joyce shifted beside me on the lumpy fifties sofa bed we bought at Goodwill. I felt her stare at me but kept my eyes pinned on the circling helicopters of M *A *S *H *. I shoved soggy orange rice to the edge of my plate. Joyce had made enchiladas and Mexican rice as a special treat for my birthday.

"You were in such a rush to leave this afternoon, Maggie," Kathy went on, "that you wouldn't even wait till I got my shoes on. So where did you go with gorgeous Blikk? His place?"

"Look, Kathy," I snapped, "I had lunch with him. Period. No way did I go anywhere with him this afternoon."

"Right! Well, whether you did or not, he seems to have taken your mind off that lost cause in Massachusetts."

"Lost cause!" I howled and jabbed my elbow into her ribs so hard that her plate flipped off her lap and onto the sofa. Enchilada sauce and rice spattered everywhere. But she was right! Kathy was right! Dear God, I might as well face it. I had lost Doug!

Joyce grabbed a towel off the clothesline that stretches across our entire living room and began mopping up the mess.

"I have to sleep on this bed, remember? Honestly, what a pair of infants! I'm thinking of looking for a couple of new roommates. Adults. People like sweet little Lupe, for instance. Too bad she moved out to marry Eddy."

Kathy snorted. "Too bad is right! That religious jerk!

22

Imagine, making her give up ballet just to marry him! I'd never do that! I'll never stop dancing as long as these dumb feet of mine hold up. Except if dreamy Armando asked me to," Kathy added, smirking at Joyce, another of Armando's ex-girlfriends. "But then, he'd never demand such a stupid thing, would he, Joyce?"

I sighed. No, Armando wouldn't, but how about Doug? Joyce just went on scrubbing the sofa. Then she collected our plates. Before carrying them into the kitchen, though, she poked her face between the limp pink legs of a pair of tights waggling from the nylon line. We have it cluttering up the living room because the bathroom is too small and too damp to dry clothes.

"And for your information, Kathy," Joyce said, "Maggie's right. She wasn't with Mr. Eriksen this afternoon. He had a meeting in Randall's office beginning at one o'clock. He was still there when I left at five."

Kathy shrugged and bent forward to poke at her foot. "My bunions are killing me! And look at this toenail. Thick and black and split clear to the cuticle. And I ache all over after Martina's class this morning. Pain. Pain. Pain. Sometimes I wonder if ballet is worth it!"

"Go take a hot shower," Joyce called from the kitchen. "Or a cold one," she added, just as our buzzer gave a thin, shaky rasp. Someone was at the street door.

"Since you're up," Kathy called to Joyce, "you get it."

"Would you, Joyce?" I asked, trying to concentrate on M *A *S *H *. "I'm sore all over too. Besides, I'm not expecting anybody."

"As I said," Joyce muttered, trudging barefoot toward the intercom, "I'm on the lookout for a couple of grown-up roommates."

Her voice became impersonal when she spoke into the tube. "Yes?"

Then, although the words croaked hollowly through the intercom, I understood them perfectly. And, dear God, recognizing the voice, I grew dizzy and breathless and

23

knew that today's fifth important event was about to take place.

"I want to see Mag. Is she there? This is Doug Anderson."

Chapter Four

"For gosh sakes! How can I ask him up here?" I cried, hearing Doug's voice on the intercom. I gestured wildly. "Look at this mess! Tell him to wait, Joyce!"

"She says wait a minute, Doug. You're just in time for the birthday cake I baked for her. How've you been?"

I kicked a pair of Kathy's dirty socks and one of her big cloddy shoes under the sofa bed. I yanked a couple of Joyce's C-cup bras off the drying line. From the coffee table I gathered up empty Tab cans and the melted ice pack I had been using on my tired left ankle.

"Here," I said, thrusting everything into Joyce's arms.

"Thanks a lot!" she said. "Shall I tell him to come up now?"

"No-o-o!" I howled, looking at the smear of enchilada sauce on my T-shirt. I pulled it off, jerked a clean one down from the line, and drew it over my head.

"Wow," Kathy drawled. She sprawled so low on the sofa bed that she was practically sitting on her shoulder blades. The big bone at the back of her neck protruded against the ratty mohair upholstery. "Two gorgeous men in one day! But it looks as if Doug's zapped Blikk Eriksen clear out of the picture!"

I whirled to stare at her. Could she be right? I mean, Blikk was sweet and smooth and, well, glamorous, and lunch with him had been exciting. But Doug! Dear God, I'd gone with Doug since high school. And now, now he had come back to me.

"How do you expect him to come up here when you're lying there in nothing but your underwear, Kathy?"

Her dingy, stretched-out bra barely covered her breasts, which were large for a dancer. Her chartreuse bikini briefs tinted her skin a paler shade of the same color.

Kathy shrugged. "This almighty Doug of yours'll only have eyes for you, roomie. Or if he happens to look my way, he'll just think I'm wearing a teeny weenie bikini."

"He will not!"

"So, toss me a towel off the line."

I groaned. "I give up. I'll simply meet him downstairs."

Pushing my feet into loafers, I grabbed a sweater and raced out the door.

"What about your birthday cake?" Joyce called just before the door slammed behind me, but I kept on going.

A few steps above the ground floor, my feet stopped along with my heart. I slapped hand to head. Good grief, I'd forgotten to comb my hair. It was exploding like the burning bush in the Bible. What would Doug think? And what if he had gotten tired of waiting and left already? My darling Doug gone! I couldn't stand the thought and, crossing my fingers, took the three remaining steps in one jump.

Swinging open the glass inner door to the small vestibule, I caught my breath. Who could even think of Blikk when Doug was standing there? Towering, rather. Even taller than I remembered. All in white. White jeans. White shirt open at the throat. Sleeves rolled up to show his mounded forearms. Wide shoulders. Narrow, narrow waist that I wanted instantly to fling my arms around. Curly hair bleached blonder by the sun although summer was only beginning. Blue eyes in a long, tapered face already tanned. Lips, smooth and full, that my fingers and mouth trembled to touch. A long shiver ran through me. But something was missing.

"Doug! You've shaved off your bushy red beard!"

He smiled a little, only a little. I saw his Adam's apple bob up and down and his hands clench behind his back. So I knew he was nervous too. But why couldn't he at least raise his hand in that jaunty salute I remembered so well? Then the dead tone of his voice when he said, "Hi, Mag," reminded me of how really terrible things were between us. I mean, nothing had actually changed since last summer when his orange sports car skidded away from my house and around the corner. His rotten birthday card should have told me that. So I didn't reach up and kiss his smooth mouth or wrap my arms around his narrow waist like I wanted to. No. I backed away.

"Uh, hi, Doug."

"I hope you don't mind my coming, Mag." His words thudded out like chunks of lead. "I'm between summer jobs and stopped off here to see my mother. So, since I was this close . . ."

"Sure, thanks for coming."

"Could we maybe go somewhere and talk?"

"Sure, I guess so."

He held open the outer door until I had passed through it, then thrust his hands into his pockets and strode off toward Geary Boulevard. I trotted along beside him like his puppy dog, for gosh sakes, taking two steps to each of his in order to keep up.

"Where's your car?" I asked, to say something. "The orange one."

"Sold it last August right after—" He broke off. "Anyway, I needed the money. MIT's expensive, even with the scholarships I'm getting there. And how are things with you?" he asked, lifting an eyebrow and a corner of his mouth. He sounded sort of snide, didn't he? Was he maybe hoping, expecting my life to be in shreds without him?

"Absolutely terrific," I said. "Things couldn't be better."

"Glad to hear it. Did you get the birthday card I sent?" He slowed his pace, actually faced me, and smirked.

"Yes. This morning. Thanks."

He gave a hoot of laughter. "Don't mention it. Is this restaurant all right? La Fleur Bleu?" He barged straight in, gave me no time to answer. Clenching my fists, I followed. I just hoped the rude waiter wasn't working tonight.

27

What if he mentioned that I had been there this noon with Blikk? Courteous, silver-eyed Blikk. But now Doug's eyes, blue and gold-flecked, shone across the table at me.

"What are you going to have?" Doug asked.

"I just finished dinner."

"Have some dessert, then. A piece of birthday cake since you're missing the one your roommate baked." He grinned. His Adam's apple bobbed, reminding me of the day I first met him. He had been a high-school junior then, I a mere freshman, swooning at his resemblance to the Greek god in our social science book. Now, with that mass of dark blond hair curling above his lean, strong face, he looked more godlike than ever. But he sure wasn't acting like a god!

"I forgot, though," he said, his grin still needling me, "ballerinas don't eat desserts, do they?"

I didn't smile. I pressed my lips together. "I've told you a hundred thousand times, Doug, 'ballerina' is a term for a star, a principal dancer. I am not a ballerina! Not yet."

The maître d' lit our candle. In its light the yellow rosebuds on our table shone like satin. When we left, would Doug think to present them to me like Blikk had? Knowing Doug, probably not. But couldn't he at least stop being so cranky?

Across from me he picked up the menu and frowned at it. He didn't hum like he used to. His stubby, straw-colored lashes hid his eyes. But I knew them by heart. Deep, deep blue, swimming with sunny flecks like tiny goldfish. Oh, Doug, Doug! Look at me and smile!

His big hands tightened on the long, vertical menu. Large hands, strong and suntanned. I trembled, remembering their touch.

The waiter who took Doug's order was a stranger, thank heavens. Doug asked for steak and salad and a glass of red wine. No quiches or delicate potato omelets for him!

"And for you, miss?" the waiter asked.

"Nothing, thanks."

"A glass of wine, perhaps?"

Before I could answer, Doug laughed. "Not Mag! She's still a child! Not old enough according to California law."

Furious, I gripped my napkin. "No wine, thank you," I told the waiter, "but please bring me a cup of coffee. Black," I added crisply. I tilted my chin toward Doug. Just let him make a crack about my taking coffee without cream or sugar!

He said nothing. One hand rocked a spoon back and forth on its bowl. He leaned forward, raised his pale lashes, and looked directly into my eyes. I gazed back, caught by his blue iris, gold-flecked, and by his glinting black pupils.

"We aren't getting off to a very good start, are we, Mag?"

My lips trembled. Tears sprang to my eyes. I shook my head, afraid my voice would break if I answered aloud.

"When I first saw you come leaping down the stairs tonight, Mag, I wanted to take you in my arms."

"Oh, why didn't you, Doug?"

He gave a quick lift to his shoulders. "Well—well, you started in with that nasty remark about my bushy beard."

"It wasn't nasty. At least, I didn't mean it to be."

"It sounded nasty to me. So I decided—well, I don't know—I decided maybe you'd met somebody else. Especially after all this time not hearing from you."

"But I don't have your address. You never wrote to me, either."

"Then you didn't ask me in."

"But the apartment's a mess. My roommates weren't dressed. Besides, there's no place to talk. Just the living room and kitchen and the one tiny bedroom."

"You're not answering my question, Mag, about meeting somebody else."

For a second I remembered Blikk's eyes shining across the table at me this noon. Flattering, but now, with Doug looming opposite me, I could think only of him.

"There's nobody else," I said softly, blinking down at my hands. "What about you, Doug?"

Before he could answer, the waiter was there with Doug's

food and my coffee. When we were alone again, Doug leaned toward me.

"There's nobody else for me, either. Not that I didn't try after you sent me packing last August. Before the workload got too heavy, I took out a lot of girls. One even had green eyes and red hair like you, but she wasn't exasperating the way you are. Didn't make me want to shake her and at the same time make love to her."

"Thanks a lot."

"I can't help it, Mag. That's what you do to me. Like tonight, sashaying down the stairs, hardly saying a word. I wanted to wring your little neck. And grab and kiss you so hard, you'd come to your senses!"

I flushed. "Well, what about you? 'Hi, Mag,' you say. Not hugging me. Not touching me. Not even shaking my hand. Just shoving your own hands into your pockets and taking off down the street. Saying you'd decided you'd better drop by since you were in the vicinity. Like you were paying a duty call on some old aunt, for gosh sakes!"

"That wasn't what I meant."

"It's what you said, wasn't it? Then that crack about ballerinas not eating desserts. Not to mention the smirk when you asked if I'd received that stupid birthday card."

"It wasn't a smirk. I just wondered if it had arrived."

"Yes, but I didn't exactly appreciate the message. The way you changed it to '*Don't* Stay on your toes'! I have news for you, Doug. I intend to stay on my toes!"

"Fine. The card was supposed to be a joke. But then, you never did have much of a sense of humor where ballet was concerned."

I bent my head. Tears spilled down.

"It's my life, Doug. I can't stop dancing."

He reached warm hands across the table and laid them over mine. "Honey, honey," he said, "I never asked you to stop dancing. Only to dance in Boston instead of San Francisco."

I found an old wadded-up tissue in a pocket of my jeans, dabbed it at my tears, and looked across the roses at him. At the frown above his blue eyes. At the glint of his teeth shining in the candlelight. At his pale, smooth lips that I had kissed so many times. My insides dissolved. "Oh, Doug! Doug!"

"That's why I had to come tonight, Mag," he went on, "to ask the same thing I asked last summer. Marry me and come to Boston."

I pulled my hands from beneath his. I shook my head. "I can't. I just can't. I have to dance."

"I told you, Mag, you can join the Boston Ballet. They'll snatch you up."

"They won't. They probably don't have any openings. And even if they did, graduates from their own school would get priority. Ballet companies are hard to get into. And I've got a start here. People know me. Like my dancing. One choreographer's even giving me a role in a new ballet he's doing this summer."

"All right. We can stay here this summer, then, if being in this ballet is so important to you. I'll find a job in Silicon Valley. Not go on up north like I planned. Then late in August we'll head east in time for the fall semester at MIT."

I hunched my shoulders. My chest felt banded with steel.

"It would be the same thing then as now. I can't give up dancing."

"For crying out loud! You wouldn't have to. Even if you don't get into a company right away, you could work part-time and—"

"At McDonalds, I suppose."

"Let me finish, Mag. You could work—not necessarily at McDonalds—and on the side take ballet lessons."

"Lessons! Doug, I'm a dancer. At nineteen I can't just take lessons. I have to dance in a company. It's now or never!"

"Trouble is, Mag, you don't love me enough!"

"That's not true. And how about you? If you love me so darned much, come back to Berkeley. It's a great school. What's so much greater about MIT?"

"The special engineering program I'm in. The terrific scholarships I have there and didn't have here."

"But I've got a good start in dancing here, Doug."

He shrugged. "So it's the old impasse again. But we love each other, Mag. Come to Boston. Give it a try," he said, then glanced up at the waiter, who paused by our table. Only it wasn't the waiter. With a gasp I saw that it was Blikk Eriksen. Blikk smiled.

"Good evening, Maggie. So you come to La Fleur Bleu twice in a single day."

My face flamed. Doug's stiffened and lengthened.

"Uh, Blikk, this is an old friend of mine, Doug Anderson. Doug, meet Blikk Eriksen, the famous Norwegian choreographer."

Doug rose barely half an inch off his chair to shake the hand Blikk offered.

"Anderson. Eriksen. A fellow countryman?" Blikk asked.

"My parents came from Sweden," Doug muttered. Grunted, really. So rude! I could have died!

"Ah, a Swede. But in this country we are no longer rivals but friends and fellow admirers of Maggie Adams, are we not? Now, if you will excuse me . . ."

"With pleasure," Doug said, glaring after Blikk.

"Jerky Norwegian! Talks like he's reciting Shakespeare or something. And the way he looks at you! I thought you said there wasn't anybody else!"

"There isn't. There isn't. I'm just going to be in his ballet."

"Right! Is that why you turned as red as a beet? Why you apparently had lunch with him here today?"

"Yes. Yes, it is! We discussed his ballet. And I don't care—I simply don't care whether you believe it or not. I've had about enough of your unreasonableness and your stupid jealousy, Doug Anderson! And—and your childishness!"

Pushing back my chair, I left the restaurant and fled past clumps of people, dusty cars parked bumper to bumper against the curb, and The Lost Horizons Bar. The Lost orizons Bar. The *H* in the neon sign no longer lights up. In

32

the vestibule of my apartment house I reached into my hip pocket for my keys. Not there. I tried another pocket. Finally I found them in my sweater just as Doug, breathing hard, slammed into the entryway. He pulled me against him.

"No! Let go."

But his lips came down on mine. At first I strained and twisted in his arms but gradually grew soft and quiet and began kissing him back. A sweetness flowed through me. And a delicious trembling. I clung to him, forgetting where I was.

But as suddenly as he had grabbed me, he released me. Off-balance, I staggered against the row of brass mailboxes. By the time they had stopped twanging, he was gone.

Chapter Five

I groped to the kitchen the next morning, slid my back down the damp, steamy wall, and slumped on the linoleum.

"Sick, Mag?" Joyce asked, pouring herself a cup of coffee.

I nodded. "Dying."

"Get back to bed, then."

But returning to bed would only bring more tossing and useless rehashing of last night's quarrel with Doug. At nine o'clock I walked to Ballet Headquarters with her and pushed myself through a two-hour warm-up. Every time I remembered Doug's kiss the clang of the brass mailboxes echoed in my ears and I would flash *piqué* turns around and around the room. Think about Blikk, you idiot! Think about his rehearsal this afternoon!

By class time I was exhausted but dragged myself through another two hours of work. After class the dressing room emptied quickly. Even Kathy took herself off, explaining, "If I rush, maybe I'll run into Armando at the deli."

Soon I was the only one left. Sighing, I swallowed my yogurt, then stretched out on a wooden bench. I slept, but my nap was a jumbled nightmare about Doug. I woke up stiff, my temples aching, and more tired than when I went to sleep. What time was it? The clock above the mirror said five minutes to one. Blikk's rehearsal began at one-thirty. I pulled on leg warmers, retwisted my hair into its topknot, then sat on the floor and flapped my knees up and down to stretch my turnout.

I didn't want to show up for Blikk's rehearsal too early. Not too late, either. So, allowing time to warm up, I shouldered my satchel at one-ten.

Joyce wasn't at her desk. Since she works a half day Saturday, she gets Wednesday afternoons off. Maude, a woman from a temporary employment agency who rinses her gray hair blue, replaces her.

I waved at Maude, climbed the stairs, and ambled toward the assigned studio. I heard footsteps behind me. Blikk's? No. A stranger's. But the man looked familiar. Dark-skinned, sturdy, straight black hair. Not a dancer. I could tell by the way he thumped along, his whole body lurching. At the double doors of each studio he stopped and put an eye to the long, thin opening where the edges didn't quite meet.

Eddy. It was Eddy, the man my friend Lupe married last summer. Before the ceremony her huge dark eyes had peered at me through her bridal veil. She handed me the St. Christopher medal Eddy wouldn't let her wear anymore. "Keep it, *cariña,* to remember me by."

What was Eddy doing here? He hated ballet. He had forced Lupe to give it up.

Thick and muscular in a striped blue suit, he came closer now. His hair slanted back from a scowling forehead and folded like a pair of crow's wings around the nape of his neck. His concave nose swooped between eyes as shiny and black as beetles. In the hollow beneath his high left cheekbone a nerve throbbed as regularly as a pulse.

He was about to pass me. "Aren't you Eduardo Salazar? Eddy?" I asked.

His scowl deepened. He squinted at me, then grunted.

"And you're Maggie, the girl Lupe keeps talking about. I'm looking for Lupe. Where is she?"

He didn't smile, although I remembered he used to smile a lot. Smile even when there was nothing to smile about. Old Smiley, Joyce used to call him.

"Is Lupe supposed to meet you here?" I asked.

Frowning, he flung out his wrist as if he'd like to hit me with it. "Listen, don't play dumb with me."

I backed away. Why was he growling at me? His face reminded me of masks I've seen in Indian museums. I glanced down the corridor. Why didn't Blikk come?

I curled one hand around the cold doorknob behind me. Should I go in? But what if nobody was there yet and Eddy followed me in? He was not much taller than I. Bulkier, though, with a body shaped like a short, thick pillar. Threatening. I mean, I didn't want to be alone with him.

"Look, Eddy," I said, trying to steady my voice, "I'm telling you the truth. I haven't seen Lupe since the night you got married."

"You're lying. She'd run straight to you. She thinks you're her best friend when really you're her worst enemy. You kept her from knowing the Lord."

My eyes widened. "Me?"

"Yeah. You and dancing."

He glowered. His eyes seemed to sink deeper into sockets edged with charcoal. My father, who happens to be a doctor, calls this dark pigment nature's eye shadow. He says it's common among people born in the tropics. It protects their eyes from the bright sunlight. Eddy's parents came from Mexico, same as Lupe's and Armando's.

Eddy's dark-rimmed eyes pinned me to the wall. Below the dip of my leotard my shoulder blades pressed against the cold plaster. I glanced down the corridor again. Empty except for somebody's old curled-up canvas ballet slippers. Silent, too, except for the pounding of several pianos and a ballet master shouting, "*Croisé devant*, if you please, ladies and gentlemen." I shivered in a draft that crept along the wall.

"I thought she'd forget you. Take the Lord into her heart," Eddy continued, "but she hasn't."

"Did—did Lupe say she was coming here?" I asked.

"No, but where else would she go? She's not at home. Not at her folks', either. I went there. Searched the entire house. Looked in every closet. Behind every door. Under every bed. Only the old woman was there. *Mi suegra!* My mother-in-law. '*Diablo!*' she screams, and hammers her fists against my chest. '*No está! No está!*'"

36

"But you can't just go around breaking into people's houses like that," I cried.

"Why not? I have a right, a duty. She's my wife. But she wasn't at her folks'. Not at your apartment, either. I checked that out too."

I stared at him. "What? You mean, you walked into our apartment?"

"Sure. Lupe used to live there, didn't she? Still has the keys."

"But that's against the law!"

"So? What are you going to do? Call the cops?"

His eyes blazed at me. I bit my lip and glanced down the corridor again. Empty. What should I do?

"Well, uh, Eddy, maybe she's back at your house by now. Maybe she just went down to the store for a minute or to visit a friend."

"She hasn't got any friends. The Lord and I are all she needs. And she didn't go to the store unless it took her all night! I haven't seen her since dinnertime yesterday. She wouldn't go to prayer meeting with me afterward. Too tired, she said. Well, what does she expect? Not eating. Last night she just pushed her food around her plate. Not that she ever does eat. Or, if she does, she sneaks to the bathroom and pokes a finger down her throat to make herself barf."

I caught my breath. "Then she has anorexia again."

He gave me a sour smile. "Correct! You got it, sweetheart! She's down to less than seventy pounds. I try to make her eat. Like last night. 'Lupe,' I said, 'you don't eat, you'll wind up back in the hospital!' Then, when I came home from church, she's gone."

"Gone?"

"Yeah. I step in the door. The apartment's neat, neater than for a long time. Dishes washed. Clothes put away. Empty, though. No note. I call the police. They can't help. 'Wait twenty-four hours,' they say, 'then file a missing persons report if she hasn't cooled off and come back by then.' Then they really crack up, laugh like maniacs. They think it's all a big joke. Some little fight we had."

I looked at his beetle eyes and the little nerve popping in the hollow of his cheek. I hunched my shoulders against the chill that ran through me.

"Uh, so did you maybe have a fight?" I asked.

He brushed away my question with a flip of his wrist. "No. We never fight. She just stares at me with those big wet eyes of hers. Now she's gone, run away, but I'll find her. And you're going to help me," he added, moving toward me. "Where's she hiding? In which room? This one? Out of my way."

He reached around me and grabbed the doorknob. I leaped to the center of the corridor. I mean, if he insisted on entering, I sure didn't want to be trapped in the empty studio alone with him!

"What the devil is going on down there?" someone shouted from the top of the stairs.

Looking around, I saw Blikk Eriksen striding toward me. Oh, thank heavens! I ran to him. "Oh, Blikk, I'm so glad to see you!" I wanted to fling myself into his arms.

He must have seen my fear. He put an arm around me. I snuggled against him and calmed down for the first time since my fight with Doug last night. Together Blikk and I faced Eddy.

"I have a right to be here," Eddy said, thrusting out his chest. "My wife's in there. I'm going in and take her home where she belongs."

"But I told you, Eddy," I said, feeling brave with Blikk's arm holding me. "Didn't I tell you? Lupe isn't here."

"I'm looking, anyway," Eddy said, and twisted the doorknob.

"Certainly. Please do," Blikk said quietly. "But I assure you, young man, there is no person by that name in the cast of my ballet. What was it again? Lupe?"

"As if you didn't know," Eddy snarled. "Lupe! Guadalupe Salazar. Now I'm going in and have me a look round."

He flung the door open with so much force that it banged against the studio wall.

Four dancers looked up, startled. Kathy, Paul, Seth, and Armando. So I wouldn't have been alone with Eddy after all. Lupe, of course, wasn't in the room.

"You see!" I cried. "I told you, Lupe's not here."

But Eddy swaggered farther into the room. He peered behind each double door, into the corners, toward the wall of mirrors that gleamed under the fluorescent ceiling lamps, and at the four dancers sprawled along the *barre* on the far side of the studio.

"Any of you seen my wife, Lupe Salazar?" he growled.

"Don't know nobody by that name, man," Armando said with a slow, insolent twang and in street language that he almost never uses. At least, not around Ballet Headquarters. His black eyes glinted, but his compact, muscular body remained draped against the *barre*. "Used to be a sweet little chick around here named Lupe Herrera, but she up and married some Chicano punk."

Eddy stiffened, and I remembered that the two of them nearly fought last year at my birthday party at my parents' house. Now Eddy stalked toward Armando.

"If you know where my wife is, you better tell me."

Armando shrugged, but his muscles tightened. "Like I said, man, I ain't seen her for more than a year."

"Because if I find out you know . . ." Eddy continued, as if he hadn't heard Armando.

Blikk stepped between them. "I believe it is time for you to leave, Mr. Salazar."

Eddy charged straight into Blikk. "Out of my way, *bolillo!*" Blikk seized Eddy's shoulder and spun him around.

"Out, I said, before I call the security guard."

Armando slid to Blikk's side. "Need any help, boss?"

Keeping his eyes fixed on Eddy's face, Blikk shook his head. "Thank you, no."

Eddy flung off Blikk's hand. "All right. All right. I'm going. But I'll be back."

Chapter Six

"Never did like that dude," Armando said after Eddy had pounded out of the studio. "I don't blame Lupe for splitting."

"But she could be sick," I said. "I'm really worried."

"Don't be," Armando said. "Let me comfort you. Come here, *pelirrojita*."

Armando dubbed me *pelirrojita* last summer when Joyce introduced us. It means "little redhead" in Spanish.

He laughed now as I backed out of his reach. His black eyes flashed beneath the red bandanna he had rolled up and tied around his head to keep sweat out of his eyes.

"I just try to help pretty girls, you know, boss," he said, grinning at Blikk. "So far, Maggie's the only holdout."

Kathy grunted. "Talk about egos!"

Armando extended his hand to Blikk. "Armando Flores at your service, Mr. Eriksen. Quite an introduction to City Ballet Company. Things aren't always this exciting!"

Blikk smiled slowly and shook Armando's hand. "I was beginning to think they were." His eyes turned silvery, and he added gently, "Exciting whenever Maggie is present."

His sweetness warmed me, filled me with a pleasant tingling that was almost happiness in spite of having lost Doug again. This time forever.

"Well, it wasn't my fault that Eddy came here. I just hope Lupe's okay," I said.

"So do we all, Maggie," Blikk said, then glanced toward the door. "Ah, here you are, Natalie."

"Darling!" she exclaimed. Like a bird ready for flight, she perched on high heels in the doorway, waiting to make her entrance. Then, with the scent of her perfume preceding her, she limped across the springy floor covering. At the center of the room she and Blikk met and kissed. Kissed! Oh, just cheeks. But how had they become such good friends in such a short time? I mean, Blikk had been here only a few days!

"That man's a fast worker, faster than me!" Armando said, draped against the *barre*.

Maybe Natalie Harper heard him. Or maybe she recognized him as the man who had carried her out of the classroom yesterday. Her glance lingered on him before Blikk escorted her to a chair in front of the mirrors.

"Harpy!" Kathy muttered beside me. "Natalie Harpy!"

"So, ladies and gentlemen," Blikk said, smiling first at Natalie, then at the rest of us, "I believe we are nearly ready to begin. First, however, I would like you to introduce yourselves. I had the pleasure of meeting Armando a few minutes ago and already know Maggie."

"Everybody knows Maggie, darling," Natalie Harper said.

"See what I mean," Kathy hissed. "A real harpy."

I bit my lip. But either Blikk hadn't heard Natalie's remark or chose to ignore it.

"Of course, I have seen everybody either in class or in studio performances," he said, "but I need to fit faces to the names on the cast list."

He opened a thick notebook that lay on top of the piano. No pianist had arrived, so Blikk must not intend to use music today.

He glanced at Kathy. "Are you Kathy Miller? I saw you dance with the *corps* in *Les Sylphides*."

"Yeah, a sylph in a woodland glade, that's me."

Blikk smiled. "I liked your dancing, Kathy. It has a lovely spriteliness. Where did you study?"

Kathy blushed and wriggled her shoulders. Underneath her flipness she's really quite shy.

"Here, Mr. Eriksen. For ten years. Same as everybody else. Except Armando. He's one of those naturals who don't have to study. A year of dance classes at U.C. Berkeley. A few lessons at Maggie's old school down the peninsula, and eureka, an apprenticeship!"

Twined like a vine along the *barre*, Armando raised his shoulders and hands in an exaggerated shrug. "What can I say? The exception that proves the rule, that's me!"

Chuckling, Blikk turned to Paul and Seth. "That leaves you two. Who is Paul and who is Seth?"

"Seth's the redhead," Paul said, smiling at the slender man beside him. "And I'm known as that tall blond."

I glanced quickly at Paul, my friend ever since I came to Ballet Headquarters as a scared scholarship student. Yes, Paul is tall and muscular. Not as tall and muscular as Doug, of course. Not as blond, either. I lifted my chin. Oh, forget Doug!

Smiling at Seth, Blikk said, "So we have two redheads in the cast. Maggie and Seth."

"*Dos pelirrojos*," Armando said, grinning. "Rare birds but not a pair. Their hearts belong to others."

Seth blushed and smiled at Paul. They're a pair, all right. But not Doug and me. Not anymore. Tears filled my eyes.

Blikk continued smiling. "Now that we know each other, let me tell you about my ballet. Or, to be more accurate, let me tell you about my idea for a ballet. For I hope you will help me create it."

"You mean, you haven't got it all figured out yet?" Kathy asked.

He nodded. "I seldom work this way, but since you young Americans are probably more familiar with rock than I am, I plan to try something new. New for me. I shall turn on the tape deck and let you dance. Afterward I hope to incorporate some of the things I see into *The Volcanoes*."

"Sounds like we do the creating," Kathy piped.

Natalie Harper sniffed. "You'll just be shuffling around, darling, while Blikk selects and edits."

"And, Maggie," Blikk said, "while you are 'just shuffling around,' as Natalie describes it, I would like you to imagine yourself as an enthralled young rock fan and assist me in developing the principal role."

I caught my breath. A lead in Blikk's ballet? Me? A mere apprentice?

But then he added, "I want your help in creating the character so that when Miss Harper's tendon is better, all she will have to do is take over the role."

"Oh." I drooped. I felt as limp as my old Raggedy Ann doll. I mean, one second, I was the star; the next, I wasn't. I turned away, not wanting Blikk to notice my tears.

A moment later rock music exploded into the room. I looked around. There was Blikk bending over the tape deck. Beside him, Natalie pressed her hands to her ears and grimaced at him. He laughed. Typical joke between adults! My parents are always putting down rock music too.

"All right, ladies and gentlemen," he called above the music, "let me see what you can do."

At first I wasn't in the mood. I stood around. Soon the music filled me, though. Forgetting Doug, Blikk, and the starring role I didn't get, I swayed and swiveled to the beat. Once or twice I noticed Blikk scribbling in his fat, loose-leaf notebook. Mostly I just strutted and shimmied, pranced and spun.

After about an hour Blikk shut off the tape.

"Interesting," he said. "You have given me much to think about. That will be all for today. Thank you very much."

I grabbed my towel and leg warmers off the *barre* and crowded toward the door with the other kids. Before I was out of the room, however, Blikk called me back. I pretended not to hear, but he raised his voice. "Miss Adams, I want a word with you, please."

I waited in the doorway, watching the others continue

down the corridor. Natalie came up with Blikk and hovered at his shoulder. Her heavy perfume nearly suffocated me.

"Maggie, I am sorry if I led you to believe, even for a moment, that you were to dance the lead," Blikk said. "You are a lovely dancer but—"

"But inexperienced," Natalie said, finishing for him. "Running into me yesterday was just that, darling. Inexperience."

I pressed my lips together. "I did not run into you, Miss Harper."

"Ladies, please," Blikk said. "I am trying to explain, Maggie, that I cannot give you the lead because, for one thing, Larry Randall insists that a ballerina head the cast. He believes people come to ballets to see principal dancers, a view I do not necessarily share. But I do believe that a ballerina, especially one as great as Miss Harper, brings to the stage an aura, a presence achieved not only by talent but also by experience."

Nodding, trying to keep from crying, I backed away and headed for the door but not before I saw the Harpy clasp one of his arms in both of hers.

"Why, thank you, darling! An utterly charming compliment from an utterly charming man!"

I stumbled out the door.

"Be so kind as to wait a minute, Maggie," Blikk called.

Hunching my shoulders, I stopped. *Please God, don't let me cry.* If Blikk touched me, circled a gentle arm around my shoulders, I would break into tears. But he stood just close enough for me to smell his pungent after-shave lotion. Natalie had the grace to linger behind in the doorway. Or perhaps he had asked her to let him speak to me alone.

"Maggie, forgive me for upsetting you. I know that what I am offering is less than you want. But perhaps you would like to understudy the role after Natalie takes it over."

Biting my lip, I nodded. Not that I was overjoyed to

44

understudy the part! Understudying it was better than nothing, though. Turning away, I scurried toward the stairs. Behind me, Blikk and Natalie laughed. About me? Maybe not, but they were carrying on together the way my parents do when they think my behavior is hilarious.

"Hi!" chirped a clear, small voice when I had nearly reached the stairs.

I glanced down. From a partly open studio door grinned a narrow, sharp-chinned face. Bright red hair framed it. Round brown eyes gleamed between lashes even more orange than mine. Now skinny shoulders appeared and the scrawny body of a girl about ten. She must have been a student in one of the summer session classes.

"You're Maggie Adams, aren't you? I'm Cammy Smith. Actually Cameo. Can you believe a mom calling her kid that?"

I couldn't help laughing at the funny little thing.

Her staccato bursts continued. "And, Maggie, you're the greatest! My very favorite dancer in the whole entire world!"

Her white face turned nearly as red as her hair, and she ducked back into the classroom.

"Well, Maggie, quite a fan you have there!" Blikk Eriksen said as he and Natalie Harper passed me. She gave a shriek of laughter. He took her arm to help her down the stairs. Help her! I mean, hadn't she gotten herself up the steps without his help?

I followed them down slowly, then remembered Eddy. I headed for Joyce's desk. But, seeing blue-haired Maude, I remembered that Joyce wasn't there. She has Wednesday afternoons off and must have been out shopping when Eddy invaded our apartment. Maybe she was home now, though, so I phoned to warn her that he might show up again.

"Don't worry, Mag," she said. "I can handle Old Smiley. But hang on a minute, somebody's at the street door."

"Be careful. It could be Eddy," I said, but she was

45

gone. I waited. A few minutes later she came back, breathless.

"Mag, it's Lupe. She's on her way upstairs. She sounded weird, really bizarre over the intercom. Can you come over here right away?"

Chapter Seven

"Heavens, what's up now?" Kathy asked as I sped into the dressing room. She lay on her back, massaging a lumpy, bruised foot.

"Lupe's at our apartment," I said, peeling off my sweaty practice clothes and struggling into jeans and sweatshirt. "She's acting strange, Joyce says. I've got to get there before Eddy does."

"But he's her husband."

"Some husband! I could never figure out why she married him."

"She loved him, silly."

"Maybe love isn't enough then," I said, hunching my shoulders and thinking of Doug.

I wriggled my feet into sandals, stuffed tights and leotard into my satchel, and headed for the door.

"See you," I called, and ran into the foyer and out the front door into the fog. It hadn't lifted all day and curtained the buildings with damp gray gauze.

I let myself into our apartment house and took the stairs three at a time to the second floor. I was about to poke my key in the lock when the door burst open. Lupe rushed toward me, then backed off. She didn't hug me the way she used to.

"*Por dios!* Hide me from Eddy. Don't let him put me in the hospital! Joyce, either. I'm not crazy like they say. Just fat."

Dirt smudged the white cotton blouse she wore outside

her skirt. Cinder-colored, it sagged unevenly inches above her new running shoes. She thrust her palms ahead of her to keep me at a distance. Her eyes, enormous and black in her ashy face, stayed watchful. Out rippled a strange giggle.

"Well, Maggie, say something!" I hardly recognized her shrill voice. "Kitty cat got your tongue?" Another giggle.

I stared. I couldn't move. Was this really Lupe? The body seemed the same, though emaciated. Her black hair, instead of falling thick and shining to her shoulders, hung matted and dull around her face. But it was her personality that stunned me. She was the flip side of quiet, gentle Lupe.

Appearing as overwhelmed as I, Joyce pressed her hands against the sofa bed behind her. Soon she shook herself and sounded too jolly.

"Look who's dropped by to see us, Mag. Little old Lupe!"

Swinging around, Lupe scowled. "I came here to hide. But Joyce wants to put me in the hospital, same as Eddy does. They think I'm crazy."

"I didn't say that, Lupe!" Joyce said.

"Sick. You said I was sick."

"Yes. I think you are."

"You see, Maggie! You see! Joyce thinks I'm crazy, but I just want to be thin. Thin as a sylph. Sylphlike. Or is it sylphish?"

Again the shrill giggle. Lupe's huge eyes flamed at me. I couldn't help backing against the door. Mad! Lupe reminded me of Giselle gone mad at the end of the ballet's first act. I had to call my father. He had been one of her doctors when she was sick before and would know what to do.

"How about having a Coke? Maybe something to eat?" Joyce asked.

Gesturing toward the kitchen, her fingers brushed Lupe's arm.

"Don't touch me! Don't touch me!" she screamed,

flinching as if she had been burned. She sprang ahead of us into the kitchen. Dear God, I had to phone my father.

"I don't eat anymore," Lupe said, "but I'll have a Coke, a diet Coke just to please you, Joyce. You, too, Maggie Paggie with the Raggedy Ann hair. Like fuzzy red yarn." A piercing giggle. "Does Raggedy Ann still sleep with you, Maggie Paggie? A doll instead of Doug? Whatever happened to Doug, anyway?"

I cringed. Oh, Lupe was sick, really sick! Then she shrieked at Joyce, who had picked up a big serving ladle. "No. No stew, I said. You weren't listening, Joyce."

For the first time I noticed the rich odor of beef and onions. A covered black frying pan steamed on our ancient, dented stove. Joyce was fixing dinner on her afternoon off for Kathy and me. She doesn't want us to get anorexia nervosa like Lupe. I shivered.

"Relax, Lupe," Joyce said. "I'm just giving the stew a couple of stirs so it won't burn." She set three diet Cokes on the Formica table. Joyce and I sat opposite each other in the nook. I slid along the circular bench to make space for Lupe. She remained standing at the end of the table, though.

"I'm staying here. Far away from everyone. Then you can't catch me. Can't catch a flea," she sang.

She popped open her Coke and took a quick swallow before setting it down. Pointing at each place setting, she counted in slow sing-song, "One. Two. Three. Four. Four plates. Four knives. Four forks. Four paper napkins. But only three people live here. Joyce. Maggie. Kathy. Who's the fourth place for?"

Joyce and I exchanged looks.

"Well, you, Lupe," Joyce said. "We hoped you'd have dinner with us. Stew used to be your favorite."

Out spiraled another high, wild giggle. "You weren't listening, Joycie. I told you, I don't eat anymore. I'm purifying myself for the Lord."

My throat went dry. "What?"

"You heard me, Maggie Paggie."

Joyce wet her lips. "Well, drink your Coke," she said. "We'll just—we'll just wait a few more minutes for Kathy."

Lupe sipped, then clanked the can on the table. Swinging her arms, she stomped up and down the kitchen. From the time she was sick before I knew what she was doing: exercising to burn calories. But then she wasn't so hostile, so strange. I mean, none of this wild giggling and babbling about purifying herself for the Lord!

I had to get hold of my father. I slid out of the nook and lifted the receiver from the wall phone. Throwing herself toward me, Lupe snatched it away.

"Oh, no. You're not phoning Eddy."

"I'm not, Lupe. I'm phoning Mama. I want to tell her about today's rehearsal. You remember how she likes to know everything about what she calls my ballet career."

Leaning close, Lupe laughed in my face. She tucked the receiver behind her back. "Liar! Liar! You explain much too much, Maggie Paggie! And your froggie green eyes shift back and forth, back and forth."

My chest tightened until I could hardly breathe. I slid onto the bench again, gulped Coke, and began coughing.

"You see? You see?" Lupe shrieked, pointing a finger at me. "You're choking. That proves you're lying." She dropped the receiver and let it swing along the wall like a pendulum. "Maggie's a liar. Maggie's a liar."

I started to retort, but Joyce put a finger to her lips. Lupe's mad giggle bubbled out.

"Lookie, lookie, Joyce is signaling Maggie to keep quiet. Joyce knows Maggie's lying too. Knows Maggie wants to phone Eddy."

"Oh, come off it, Lupe," Joyce snapped, sounding almost normal. "Eddy's the last person we want here. But how about your parents or your older brother? They should know that you're sick and need help."

Stiff-armed, Lupe leaned her palms on the table. She glared into our faces. Although she's tiny, hardly more than five feet, and now, terribly thin, she seemed to loom above us.

50

"Who's sick? I came here to hide. And you keep saying I'm sick. You're supposed to be my friends. Some friends!"

"We are your friends, Lupe," Joyce said.

"Sure we are," I said. "We love you, Lupe."

But she was no longer listening. Her head snapped around and she faced the door. "What was that noise?"

"I didn't hear anything," I said.

"Neither did I," Joyce said.

Lupe ran to the kitchen door, pressed her hands against the doorjambs, and hung between them, listening.

"Hear that? Footsteps creaking up the stairs. Eddy!"

"You're imagining things, Lupe," Joyce said. "I don't hear a sound. Nobody's coming. And it couldn't be Eddy. He doesn't have the keys."

I knew he did and so did Lupe. "He's coming to put me in the hospital," she wailed. "Where'll I hide?"

She dashed through the living room and bedroom. The bathroom door slammed, then clicked.

"She's locked herself in," I said.

Joyce and I jumped up from the table.

"What'll we do?" I asked.

"Call your dad quick."

I grabbed the swinging receiver. It emitted shrill pulsing beats from being left off the hook too long. I hung it up, lifted it again, and was waiting for a dial tone when a key grated in the lock of the living room door. Eerie! Lupe's hearing must be really acute to have heard someone coming up the stairs.

When the door swung open, Joyce exclaimed, "Kathy! It's Kathy!"

"Well, who did you expect? Dracula? I live here, remember? You're both pale as ghosts."

Joyce and I looked at each other and giggled hysterically. Joyce actually hugged Kathy, a rare event. Because of Armando, they're not exactly friends.

"I never ever expected to be this glad to see you," Joyce said. "But we've got to get Lupe out of the bathroom."

She ran ahead of us into the bedroom and between the

51

two mattresses that Kathy and I sleep on. From the bathroom came the gush of water running full-force. Joyce rapped on the bathroom door.

"Lupe, come on out."

No answer. I listened. The whole apartment listened. All I could hear was the water running and my own heart hammering.

"Lupe, unlock the door," Joyce said. "It was only Kathy coming up the stairs. Not Eddy."

Still no answer. Should I run phone my father? No, it would take him an hour to drive up here. And now we needed immediate action, not advice.

"We'll have to break down the door," I whispered.

"No, I'll get the screwdriver," Joyce said.

"Good thinking!" Kathy said, snickering nervously. "Removing the lock'll save our damage deposit."

"But that'll take too long," I said. "That water running. I don't like the sound. And what if she finds something in the medicine cabinet? Something to swallow?"

"Yeah," Kathy said, "or a razor blade."

I shuddered. "Don't even think such a thing! Let's climb in from the fire escape. Help me shove open these bars."

We stood on my mattress and shoved the accordion-folding guard to one side of the bedroom window. Climbing out, we inched along the fire escape toward the bathroom window. For a second I looked down at the street and turned dizzy. Below me the street lamps filled with light. The mist had lifted enough to see the towers of the bridge against the sunset. Foghorns howled outside the Golden Gate. That's what I felt like doing, howling.

I reached the bathroom window ahead of Kathy. Open! The grid guarding it stood pressed aside. The plastic curtains hung lifeless. The dim room yawned empty. The metal ladder of the fire escape rested in place at the second-story landing. It sinks to the street under a person's weight. Had it gone down with Lupe and returned? The water roaring in the bathroom must have drowned out the sound.

52

I scanned the street below. No Lupe. Nothing except cars parked along the curbs and, halfway down the next block, a handful of children jumping rope.

Then at the far end of the block something white skimmed along the curb just above the gutter. Lupe? A Wili? In legend and in the ballet *Giselle*, a Wili is the spirit of a dead maiden. A chill ran through me.

Chapter Eight

The white wisp, which I thought might be Lupe, blended into the fog at the end of the block.

Kathy climbed off the fire escape and back into the bedroom. I wriggled through the narrow bathroom window to shut off the faucet. Lupe must have turned it on deliberately to cover the sound of her escape. Oh, her sickness was making her crafty! I hunched my shoulders against a sudden chill.

"Come on," Joyce said after I had unlocked the bathroom door and joined her and Kathy in the living room. Leading us downstairs, she added, "We've got to find her. Mag, you and Kathy take the side street, I'll go along toward Geary."

The kids jumping rope didn't even glance up when Kathy and I passed. Maybe they thought we were joggers. Row houses and garage doors lined one side on the broad, dirty sidewalk, parked cars and empty garbage cans the other. From the next intersection we saw only more apartment fronts, more dusty cars, and a man trudging home with a briefcase.

"Maybe Lupe ducked into a doorway or turned the next corner," I said.

"A wild-goose chase, if you ask me," Kathy said.

At Geary Joyce strode toward us past The Lost orizons Bar, the delis, restaurants and dry-cleaning places. Still no Lupe, though.

Joyce shook her head. "She could be anywhere. In a

restaurant. Down the next block. She could have caught a bus.''

"Yeah, it's hopeless,'' Kathy said.

"But we've got to do something,'' I cried. "We can't let her wander around as sick as she is. Maybe we should call the police.''

Back at the apartment Joyce phoned them, listened, then hung up, sighing. "The officer on duty said the police can't do anything right now, but after she's been gone twenty-four hours, her relatives should file a missing persons report.''

My father wasn't much help, either.

"If she turns up again, Mags,'' he told me on the phone, "try to persuade her to get medical help. That'll be tricky, though. Most mentally ill people resist. Sometimes the police have to be called in.''

"But what happened to her?'' I asked. "I thought she had completely recovered from anorexia.''

"That's how her illness was diagnosed, Mags. But with mental illnesses you never know for sure. And they often recur for various reasons. Stress. Hereditary tendencies. Chemical imbalance. You name it. Best thing you can do now is notify her family that you've seen her.''

I couldn't bear to call Eddy, but I dialed her parents' house and talked to Manuel, her older brother. Her parents speak only Spanish.

"Thank you very much, Maggie,'' Manuel said in his careful English. "We have been worried about Lupe, especially after Eddy came here today and frightened my mother so badly. Lupe has not seemed herself for a long time. We will let you know if we hear anything.''

"I feel so helpless,'' I told my roommates when I hung up the phone. "If only we could do something!''

"How about having a little stew,'' Joyce said.

"I'm really not hungry,'' I said. "My stomach's churning what with Lupe and—and what happened last night. . . .'' I let the sentence trail off, but Joyce gave me a sharp glance.

"Guess I'll lie down for a while," I added, hurrying to the bedroom.

On my mattress I groped for my Raggedy Ann doll. Not on my pillow. Not between the sheets. Not on the floor.

"All right, you clowns, who took her?" I yelled at my roommates. "Who took Raggedy Ann? She's not here."

"Your pillow mate?" Kathy asked, grinning from the doorway. "Don't look at me!"

Behind her, Joyce frowned. "I wonder if Lupe . . . I remember her babbling something about Raggedy Ann this afternoon. But why would she take a doll?"

"Because she's crazy," Kathy said. "Or maybe not so crazy. Maybe she thinks it's weird for a nineteen-year-old still to be sleeping with just a doll."

"Drop dead!" I said, crawling between the sheets. "And shut off the light, will you?" After they left I hugged my pillow against my chest. Gradually it warmed me, melted me, and I got to imagining that I was in Doug's arms and that he was kissing me. I grew almost as breathless as when he had grabbed and kissed me in the clanging, echoing vestibule. I covered my ears and kicked the pillow to the floor. Think about Blikk. His silvery eyes. Dancing in his ballet!

My advice wasn't hard to follow, especially the next afternoon when Blikk bounded into our rehearsal bristling with energy.

"Good afternoon, ladies and gentlemen. I was so delighted with your work yesterday that we will begin the same way today. And, Maggie, from now on I want you to dance the young girl who comes to a rock show with a dull, uninteresting boyfriend."

"Doug?" Kathy whispered beside me, giggling.

I jabbed my elbow into her ribs. "Doug is not dull!"

Turning away, I pushed at my hair. Not dull at all. Stubborn. Contrary. But never dull.

"Then our young girl, our Maggie, sees the bandleader and becomes mesmerized by him," Blikk was saying. His sweet gray eyes rested on me. "Do you understand, Maggie?"

56

I nodded. Already I adored the role. If only it were really mine. If only Natalie weren't hovering around, breathing down my neck, so eager to take it over the instant her tendon got better. But at least she wasn't at rehearsal today, simpering and fanning her eyelashes at Blikk.

"If Maggie's the young girl, who's the bandleader?" Kathy asked.

"I can see that you have a candidate, Miss Miller," Blikk said, smiling.

Kathy blushed. Even her scrawny neck and shoulders turned red.

"Well, how about Armando?"

Blikk glanced at Armando sprawled against the *barre*, as limp as if he hadn't a bone in his body. He didn't move, just grinned.

"Yes, I suppose a young lady might become mesmerized by Armando Flores," Blikk said, his sentence tilting at the end to form a question. "Do you think Armando Flores could mesmerize you, Maggie?" he asked, mesmerizing me himself with his silvery gaze. I looked away, blushing.

"Sure. I guess so," I said. "I mean, I could pretend he did. Aren't dancers supposed to pretend just like actresses?"

"Very well, then, Mr. Flores, we will try you as the bandleader," Blikk said, as if he had just that minute made the decision. Who else in the cast could possibly dance the role? Shy Seth? Gentle Paul?

When Blikk switched on the tape, I shimmied around Armando, but in my mind his dense black irises became Blikk's gray eyes. I smiled at Armando. My face followed his as if he were the sun and I a sunflower. It was Blikk I smiled at, though. Blikk's face that mine followed.

Suddenly a harsh laugh jolted me and broke my concentration. Into the studio minced Natalie Harper. She inclined her beautiful head toward Blikk. "Sorry to be late, darling."

Frowning, I went on dancing. Oh, I hoped she wasn't Blikk's type.

Every afternoon for the rest of the week she sidled into the studio ten, fifteen, even thirty minutes late for rehearsal. But from the second week on, she arrived on time. Had Blikk asked her to be prompt? I sure wished he had told her to stay away entirely. My insides turned cold just knowing that she was sitting there at the front of the room, knees crossed, one foot twitching, great, cold eyes following my every shimmy and spin in the role that would soon be hers.

Of course, Blikk watched me, too, but I loved his attention. Gloried in it. I danced for him. *With* him, in my imagination. And obviously he liked what he saw. He smiled and praised me a lot.

"Maggie, you look wonderful. Very strong!"

Once, after my *pas de deux* with Armando, he called, "Very expressive, Maggie. Touching. The character you are creating reminds me of one of the Lovers-in-Innocence in *Pillar of Fire*. Do you know that Anthony Tudor ballet?"

"Oh, yes," I said, gazing into his silvery eyes. I hardly thought about Doug anymore. Well, not very often, anyway.

Natalie snorted and recrossed her knees. "It's not so hard to play an innocent, darling, when one is as young and innocent as Maggie Adams. Of course, innocence isn't everything," she added, smirking at Armando.

"Harpy!" Kathy muttered beside me.

Finally, one afternoon the inevitable happened.

Blikk called me to the front of the room where Natalie sat doodling dancer's feet on a page of his notebook. My stomach lurched. Dear God, her *sur les pointes* sketches reminded me of the ostrich on Doug's birthday card!

Blikk stood up, cupped his hands around my shoulders, and looked into my eyes. Deep, deep! I trembled.

"Maggie, you know how pleased I am with the role you have created. It is so appealing. Now I would like to see if you are as good at teaching as you are at dancing. The doctors say Miss Harper is ready to dance again, so I want you to teach her the rock fan's part."

Chapter Nine

For Blikk's sake I tried to teach Natalie my role, the role that was really mine, mine and Blikk's, the role I had created while I gazed into his silvery eyes, not Armando's black ones.

At rehearsal after rehearsal I tramped through the steps with her, showed her how to swing her hips, how to shake her shoulders, how to waggle her pelvis. I really tried. And I didn't let anyone know how hopeless and empty I felt. At least, I didn't think anyone knew. Finally, one afternoon, my own ankle, the weak one, started aching.

Blikk stopped the tape. "Maggie, why are you limping?"

I stared at the floor. If I looked into his eyes, I would break into tears. "I'm—I'm sorry, Mr. Eriksen, I didn't realize I was."

"I want you to stop for today, Maggie. Go home and put ice on your ankle."

"But, really, it's all right."

"I mean it, Maggie. Go home and rest."

Pressing my lips together, I nodded.

I reached the corridor without crying and rushed downstairs past Joyce. I pretended not to hear her call, "What's wrong, doll?"

But once inside the dressing room I dropped onto the bench, slumped over, and sobbed. Oh, not about my ankle. No. About not dancing the role that was really mine. Mine and Blikk's. Then, suddenly, I realized I was crying about Doug, who was really mine too. Even if the idiot didn't know it!

Hearing someone coming, I bent over double and was rubbing my ankle when Joyce came in. She pushed a postcard at me. "For you, Mag. The mailman just brought it. You wouldn't stop when I yelled at you a minute ago."

My fingers tightened around the card. From Doug? My heart caught. I dabbed at my eyes with a tissue. Oh, please let him say he misses me. But what was this? Oil derricks marched across the card. Oil derricks? But wasn't he working somewhere in Oregon?

"Well, read it, Mag," Joyce said.

I turned the card over. Maybe these two lines with the rearing capitals said he missed me. "Having fun here in good old Gillette, Wyoming. Don't you wish you were here?"

I crushed the card in my hand. Tears poured down my face. "So darned smug! I just hate him!"

I didn't toss the card into the wastepaper basket, though. For some reason I slid it into my satchel, and instead of going straight home to our apartment, I detoured to a nearby library. In an atlas I located Gillette, in northeast Wyoming. Where Doug must be working. Not that I cared!

As soon as I got home I crawled into bed. An hour later Kathy stumbled into the room and woke me shuddering from a confused dream about Doug, oil derricks, and clanging, echoing mailboxes.

"What time is it?" I asked. "Is Joyce home yet?"

"Nope. We're on our own. She went out to dinner."

"Who with?"

"She wouldn't say. Nobody I knew, she said, really cranky. Everybody was cranky this afternoon. Including the Harpy. After you left she griped that the rock dancing bothered her tendon. 'I'm not a go-go dancer, darling!' she told Blikk. Then she insisted on wearing *pointe* shoes. She looked exactly like what she is: a classical ballerina trying to be a fifteen-year-old rock fan!"

I saw what Kathy meant at the next rehearsal. Natalie still couldn't get the loose, snaky movements of the body

60

so essential in this ballet. Her legs and arms moved fairly well now, but her body remained erect and rigid. She seemed about to start classical *développés,* for gosh sakes!

"Take a break, ladies and gentlemen," Blikk finally told us after we had repeated the same sequence at least ten times. Kathy and I followed Armando to the door.

"Please be back in half an hour," Blikk called after us. He turned to Natalie. "The hips must be relaxed," he told her. He pushed his own hips forward to demonstrate. "They should rotate like rubber. Do you see?"

"Yes, indeed. And I just love the way your hips move, darling."

I clenched my teeth and bent over the drinking fountain.

"The boss should let me show the lady how to grind," Armando said. "Privately, of course."

"Oh, privately! Privately!" Kathy mimicked. "You make me sick, Armando. You think you're so macho!"

He grinned. "You know it!"

They strolled off, still bickering while I cooled my face in an arc of water. Suddenly a little voice said, "Hi, Maggie."

Beside me squirmed Cammy Smith, the ten-year-old with the narrow, vivid face and bright red hair. Her grin showed shiny new braces.

"Look, I just got these. Someday my teeth'll be as pretty as yours. But now I have to get back to class."

She waved and skimmed a couple of *glissades* to the door of her classroom. So quick. So light. A leaf blowing in the wind. In the studio she joined a line of other skinny little girls to perform a simple *glissade, assemblé, arabesque* combination across the floor. My heart tightened. Cammy's dancing had the same lovely purity Lupe's used to have! Poor Lupe! Where was she now?

Sighing, I descended the stairs, then gave a little cry, for, outside the glass front doors, Lupe drifted past in the fog. Willow-thin. Black hair. Filmy, long white dress. Jagged hem clinging to bony calves.

"Joyce," I yelled over my shoulder. "It's Lupe. Come quick!"

Joyce was beside me in seconds. I pointed to the white blur fading into the mist at the end of the street. "There she goes."

We ran to the corner. But when we reached it, we saw in a pocket clear of fog that the girl was too tall, too big-boned. She stared as us from blue eyes set in a large pale face. A stranger.

"Sorry," Joyce told her, "we thought you were someone else."

By the time we returned to the studio, rehearsal had begun again. I slid between Paul and Seth and swung into the dance. Blikk didn't seem to notice that I was late. He was dancing hard, swinging his pelvis and shoulders. I caught my breath. He was a marvelous dancer, although he rarely performed anymore—only an occasional character role. His tutoring had failed to help Natalie, though.

"The Harpy still looks like a peasant girl from *Giselle,* not a modern rock fan," Kathy whispered in the corridor during our next rest period. "Her acting's even worse than her dancing. Nothing but simpering at Armando."

I shrugged. "Don't tell me. Tell Blikk."

Of course, she didn't, and was still complaining a few weeks later on the day before dress rehearsal. "What I hate most is her coyness. All the Harpy ever does is flap her eyelashes at Armando!"

I sniffed. "Well, Armando doesn't seem to mind. Blikk, either. In fact, Blikk seems to like the way she's doing the role."

But it turned out he didn't.

We had been rehearsing only about an hour when he glanced at his watch. "Thank you, ladies and gentlemen. That will be all for today."

I stared at him, surprised. I mean, with dress rehearsal tomorrow and the ballet still needing a lot of work, why was he dismissing us so early? I was about to go off with the others when he added, "Everybody may leave except Natalie and Maggie."

"What?" I asked, frowning.

"You are to stay, Maggie," he said.

"Well, okay. Sure."

Puzzled, I remained at the *barre*, toweled away sweat, twisted an escaping strand of hair, pulled up my leg warmers. I mean, Natalie certainly needed to rehearse, but why did he want me to stay too?

She lingered near Blikk, tightening a shawl around her narrow shoulders. He waited for the other dancers to clear the room, then asked abruptly, "Maggie, please tell us how you think the young rock fan feels when she looks at the bandleader."

Natalie laughed.

I tried to ignore her. "I—I don't understand, Blikk," I stammered. But, of course—naturally I understood exactly what he meant.

"Let me explain. When you were creating the role, Maggie, how did you evoke your mood? Your wistfulness?"

I swallowed. "I—uh—just pretended the bandleader was someone I—well—liked."

Natalie hooted. "The Maggie Adams version of the Stanislavsky method of acting!"

I bit my lip.

Blikk ignored Natalie. "Well, whatever you did, Maggie, worked beautifully," he said quietly. "Would you mind dancing for us now? The part where the fan first sees the bandleader."

He started the tape at Armando's entrance and held out his arms to me.

"Pretend that you are dancing with someone you love," he said, smiling gently. "With the handsome Swede, perhaps."

My face burned. Natalie gave a snort of laughter. A wicked smile twisted her red mouth. "She doesn't have to pretend anything, darling. She's dancing with you, the man of her dreams."

My face flaming, I ran toward the door.

"You are not to leave, Maggie," Blikk called. "Natalie is only teasing. Come, we will dance together."

He pulled me into his arms. Stiff at first, I soon melted with his strong hands guiding me. I pivoted, shook my shoulders, swung my hips, never looked away from his mesmerizing eyes.

"Wonderful, Maggie," Blikk said when we finished. "Thank you. That will be all until tomorrow at dress rehearsal."

Dazed, I gathered my towel and sweater off the *barre*. I heard him say, "Do you see, Natalie? That is how I want you to dance the role."

I floated out of the room, down the corridor, and stopped in front of Joyce at the reception desk. There I flicked my calves together at the side in a high *grande cabriole*.

"He likes my dancing," I sang. "Maybe he even likes me."

Chapter Ten

All during company class the morning before dress re-hearsal, my legs and stomach ached. So did my ankle. And I was dancing only in the *corps*. Imagine how Natalie Harper must feel, having the lead in a type of ballet she wasn't used to performing.

Her face seemed paler than usual under the harsh fluorescent glare. Her left ankle bulged with Saran Wrap, which she preferred to the more usual elastic bandage. I heard her rasp something at Martina. Once I caught her watching me and gave her a quick, nervous smile. She turned away.

I shrugged. "Is it my fault she can't do it?" I whispered to Kathy, who was dawdling through the *rond de jambe* exercise in front of me at the *barre*. Sometimes Kathy acts as if she couldn't care less about being a dancer.

"Stinks in it, you mean," she said.

"She'll ruin the entire ballet," I said. "Oh, poor Blikk!"

"Poor Blikk, my foot! Only reason he doesn't boot her out is because they have something going!"

My face flamed. "You don't know that!"

"Open your eyes, girl!" Kathy mouthed, because Martina was looking our way. Then, hunching her shoulders, my roommate added, "The Harpy's out to get Armando too."

After class and a brief lunch break I returned to the dressing room. Kathy was already there with another girl recently added to the cast. I brushed my hair, which in the ballet flows loose, then got into my costume.

"Some costumes," Kathy said. "Same thing we wear every day. Jeans and T-shirts. Low-budget, I got to admit, though. Of course, our theatre's low-budget too."

Kathy was right. When we were dressed, instead of heading to the downtown theatre where we perform *The Nutcracker* every Christmas and present our repertory season every spring, we merely climbed upstairs to the large double rehearsal hall. Our stage, Studio D, rises three steps above Studio C, where the audience sits. This afternoon the pleated divider, which usually separates the two rooms, was folded back. A theatre curtain of heavy cotton stood open when we arrived. Now increased to nine, the cast in jeans looked ready for backpacking, not performing. All except Armando. He glittered in tight, sequined pants and matching shirt. Natalie had not come in yet.

"Da-dah! A suit of light," said Armando, strutting in front of Kathy and me. "Like matadors wear to fight the bulls."

Pirouetting across the stage, he resembled a shimmering top.

Blikk Eriksen strode in with a tape deck tucked under one arm. At the sight of his bouncing step, a sliver of light as bright as Armando's suit ran through me. I gave my head a shake to clear it. My hair swirled around my face and shoulders. I skimmed, smiling, to join the cluster around Blikk.

"Are we all here?" he asked. His glance moved from dancer to dancer.

"All here except for Señorita Harper," Armando drawled. Standing with arms crossed and one instep draped over the other, he appeared as relaxed as when he lounges against the *barre*.

Blikk frowned. "Miss Harper will be here shortly. She is having her costume fitted."

Kathy snorted but not loud enough for Blikk to hear. "Why couldn't she wear jeans like the rest of us? Here she comes. Sex-cy!"

Natalie Harper hovered in the doorway in a clinging wraparound tunic. After a moment she ankled across to

Blikk and laid a hand on his arm. For once he ignored her and looked at his watch. Kathy and I exchanged grins.

Natalie took in a sharp breath, even blushed under her heavy makeup. "Sorry to be late, darling."

"Yes. Because of the costume fitting, I suppose." He sounded as if he didn't believe it.

He jumped lightly to the lower studio and sat down on a chair in the last row.

"We are ready to begin," he said, his Norwegian accent changing the sentence into a question. "Places, everybody. And, Jim," he called to a stagehand, "please shut the curtain."

Rock music blared. We danced. But the curtain remained closed.

"Jim, the curtain should open immediately after the action commences," Blikk called. "We will begin once more."

The music stopped, started, and we began again. This time the curtain opened on cue with six of us gyrating below a tall, irregular silhouette of a rock band. At its base winked lights spelling the group's name, THE VOLCANOES.

Shuffling opposite Seth, I waggled my hips and shoulders. I shook my head so hard that my hair showered around my face. We were fifteen bars into the music when Paul and Natalie made their entrance. She was the only one in the cast wearing *pointe* shoes. The music halted.

"Natalie and Paul, you were late," Blikk called. "And, Natalie, enter a little ahead of your partner. Rap the floor with your *pointe* shoes. Use them as you would tap shoes. Also throw your hips more. And, chew your gum harder. You do not particularly like this boy you are with. He bores you. He is—what was it you called him once, Maggie?"

"A wimp," I murmured. Natalie's stare sent a chill through me. But could I help it if she wasn't able to dance my role? The role I created for Blikk? With him, really.

"Speak louder, Maggie," Blikk said.

"She said 'a wimp,' " Kathy yelled. "A nerd."

"All of the above," Armando shouted from the wings

where he waited in his suit of lights. Natalie's slow gaze rested on him.

"Yes," Blikk said. "Now, from your entrance, Natalie and Paul."

Once more the music rumbled, and Natalie traipsed ahead of Paul onto the stage. Kathy raised both eyebrows at me as we rocked past each other. "What'd I tell you? A first-act Giselle," she mouthed with a nod toward Natalie.

I giggled. The music halted. I stiffened. Good grief, were we stopping because Blikk had heard me giggle? No, thank heavens!

"Natalie, please put a little more casualness into your entrance," Blikk said. "You had a word for it, Maggie."

"Laid-back," I muttered. "Relaxed."

"Yes, laid-back," Blikk said. "All right. Once more from your entrance, please, Natalie. And more, as Maggie says, laid-back." He smiled.

"Maggie this! Maggie that!" Natalie grumbled. Tiny lines sprayed from around her eyes. Excess flesh puckered her jawline. Suddenly she seemed tired and old. I mean, how could Blikk possibly love her?

Natalie and Paul tried their entrance again. Her dancing looked no better, but Blikk didn't stop them this time. Maybe he figured he didn't have all day. Randall had a dress rehearsal scheduled here at three o'clock.

Now came the bandleader's entrance. On cue Armando, in his glittering suit, sauntered on stage among the four rocking couples.

"React! Everybody!" Blikk called above the music. "Remember, he mesmerizes you, Natalie."

Armando leaped onto the riser and strutted back and forth in front of the black silhouette of the band. With the other dancers I drifted toward him, arms at my sides, face lifted to his. Then the music quit, and Blikk's clipped voice shattered my concentration.

"Take it again from the leader's entrance. And this time, Natalie, please let me see how much you long for this fellow."

"What do you think I was just doing!" she snapped. Her face turned crimson.

Blikk rewound the tape and Armando repeated his entrance. Once more the music stopped and we redid his entry. We danced this sequence three times before Blikk walked to the edge of the stage. His small, neat hands rested on it. Looking up from the lower studio, he called Natalie to him and spoke to her so quietly that only she could hear. Her sloping white shoulders drooped.

"I hope he's really chewing her out," Kathy said. "Serves her right!"

I nodded. As Kathy said, she had it coming! But somehow the droop of her shoulders touched me. I turned away.

"Very well, we will take your entrance again, Armando," Blikk said, going back to his seat.

Armando pranced to the riser a fourth time; we clustered after him, then the music quit.

"Would it help if you watched Maggie run through it once, Natalie?" Blikk asked.

My insides turned to jelly. Dear God, I couldn't! I was exhausted. I hadn't danced the role since it became Natalie's. And who was I to demonstrate for the prima ballerina?

"No, darling," she barked at Blikk. "That will not be necessary. If you want a teenybopper, then use one. Use this wonderful Maggie Adams of yours."

Silence. Natalie limped out. I froze. My heart pulsed in my throat and in my ears. Blikk's face lengthened into a narrow, sharp-nosed mask. He pivoted and returned to the back of the room. After he was seated again he called, "From Armando's entrance please. Maggie, take over the role of the young rock fan. And please do it *en pointe*."

"*En pointe?*" I asked. "But I've never done it *en pointe*."

"*En pointe,* Maggie."

"Yes. All right."

With cold, shaking hands I changed into *pointe* shoes and in sort of a dream—nightmare, maybe—danced the rest of the ballet. Armando made love to me in his suit of lights, but the eyes gazing into mine were Blikk's silvery gray ones.

69

We finished just as Randall barged on stage.

"How much longer?" he demanded.

"No longer, Mr. Director," Blikk told him quietly.
"We are through." He turned to us. "Thank you very
much, ladies and gentlemen. You all looked wonderful."

I picked up my ballet satchel and, still dazed, went
down the corridor. On either side of me, Kathy and Armando
sort of carried me along.

"Apprentice prima ballerina we should call you," Kathy
said. "Wasn't that how your ex addressed his famous
birthday card?"

It took me a minute to understand what she was talking
about.

"My ex? Doug is not my ex!" I snapped. "He's still
mine, whether he knows it or not!"

"Okay. Okay," Kathy said, raising her eyebrows at
Armando. "Take it easy, Maggie!"

Then, behind us, Blikk suddenly asked, "Maggie, may
I speak with you?"

I jumped. Had he overheard our stupid conversation?
His face remained a mask, though. I dropped back to walk
beside him.

"You understand, I hope, Maggie, that you are to dance
the young fan at the opening and until further notice.
Natalie's costume will need altering to fit you, of course."

"Natalie's tunic?" I asked. "But the rock fan should
wear jeans."

He smiled slightly. "The tunic is more feminine."

My face burned. "Uh, do you think so?" I muttered,
vowing to wear dresses everywhere from now on. Anything to please Blikk! Had Doug liked me in dresses too?
Oh, forget Doug!

"One more thing, Maggie," Blikk went on. "Although
it will be announced that you are dancing the rock fan, the
programs have already been printed, so you will not be
listed as performing that role. Your name will be associated with the young rock fan, however—your first name—
because I have named her Maggie—after you."

Chapter Eleven

Talk about an unknown stepping at a moment's notice into a starring role! From the moment Blikk told me that I was to dance the lead in his ballet, my whole body seemed made of thin blown glass ready to shatter at a touch or even a sound.

The night before *The Volcanoes* opened, I had to get up to drink warm milk in order to sleep. In the morning my fluttery stomach barely kept down toast and coffee. After company class, which Natalie skipped, thank heavens, I didn't even try to swallow my usual six ounces of yogurt. Instead I spent the lunch hour teaching my old part in Blikk's ballet to Anita. For some reason she couldn't seem to get it right.

"For gosh sakes, loosen up," I told her for about the tenth time. "And move, Anita, move!"

Only when Blikk's reflection appeared in the studio mirror and hovered in the reflected doorway did I realize that I had been yelling, really shrieking at poor Anita, who must be as nervous as I.

Facing around, I ran to Blikk.

"I'm falling apart, Blikk. Going to pieces."

He put his arms around me.

"There, there, Maggie. I will take over for you here. You are to go home, put a little ice on your ankle, and rest. Get some rest."

At his gentleness, I sobbed against his shoulder, dampening the soft, thick cotton of his sweatshirt.

71

"Oh, Blikk, I'll never ever be able to do it. I'll ruin your wonderful ballet!"

"Nonsense, Maggie. You will dance beautifully. As usual. Now follow my advice and take a rest. Come along."

He led me toward the door as Joyce entered. She flagged a card at me. "The mailman just handed it to me, doll, so I brought it right up. It's from you know who."

Blushing, I stepped away from Blikk. I thrust my hands behind my back and refused to take it.

Blikk smiled. "From your sweetheart?"

"Doug? He's not my sweetheart. I haven't seen him in ages. Not since the night . . ." I began, remembering that Blikk's stopping at our table in La Fleur Bleu had started our quarrel. Our final quarrel. I hunched my shoulders.

"They say that absence makes the heart grow fonder," Blikk said.

"Not with us. Just the opposite."

"Well, go home and rest, Maggie, and be back here at six."

I nodded, afraid that my voice would shake if I thanked him. I left without Doug's card, but Blikk came after me with it. "You forgot something, Maggie."

"Uh, thanks." I held it by the edges, as if it might burn me, and shoved it into my ballet bag. In the dressing room, though, even before I changed into street clothes, I took it out. *Oh, please say you miss me, Doug.*

On one side of the card ambled a big-shouldered polar bear that somehow reminded me of Doug. My breath caught. On the other side, postmarked Dillingham, Alaska, Doug's bold scrawl with its halo-dotted *i*'s said, "Having fun. Don't you wish you were here?"

That did it! I ripped the card into tiny pieces and dropped them into the trash can.

Ten minutes later I had just unlocked the door to our apartment when the phone rang. It was Mama calling. I had phoned her the night before to tell her I was dancing the lead in Blikk's ballet.

"We can come to see you after all, baby. I talked my

statistics instructor into letting me put off the midterm until next week. And your father persuaded his partner to take his on-call night. So we'll be there to see our very own ballerina.''

"Mama! I am not a ballerina!"

"I know, baby, but you're on your way."

I didn't feel "on my way" when I arrived at the studio a few minutes after five. *Dear God, don't let me make a fool of myself in front of everybody. Or end up not dancing at all.* Which had happened five years ago after Randall threatened to walk out if I replaced Martina in *The Nutcracker.* That night was also the only time Doug ever came to one of my performances. Maybe if he had seen me dance then or later, he would understand why ballet is so important to me. I pushed at my hair. For gosh sakes, forget Doug! Just concentrate on doing okay tonight.

I climbed upstairs to dress in a small classroom adjacent and convenient to the double studio where we were to perform. A curtain separated the men's dressing area from the women's. A handful of girls from the ballet Bob Morris choreographed before he left sat putting on makeup.

"Looks like I'm the only one here from *Volcanoes,*" I said. "I guess I'm overanxious."

"Yep! That's what you are, all right, Maggie," said one of the girls. "I sure wouldn't be here now except that we go on first. And, my gosh, *Volcanoes* is last. Looks like you're bucking for soloist or something!"

I sniffed. "Soloist! Oh, sure! I'm here because I couldn't stand hanging around the apartment a minute longer. Joyce was being motherly and, good grief, Kathy was eating canned tamales and refried beans. I mean, my stomach was already turning cartwheels! How can she eat junk like that just before performing?"

The girl snickered. "I have news for you, Maggie. Kathy's not as eager as you. Practically nobody is. You might even make it someday. Unless you have too many more run-ins with Randall."

"Oh, him!" I slumped down at one of the temporary dressing tables and, with cold, trembling fingers, unzipped my ballet satchel. "Speaking of Randall, where are his dancers? They go on second."

"Oh, they're here," said the girl at the next table. "Can you believe it? They're still rehearsing. They've been at it all afternoon, poor kids, and are ready to drop. Thank heavens I don't have to work with Randall. Lord, what if he becomes permanent director?"

"Good grief, don't even think that! My stomach's tender enough already. I'm going to go warm up."

"Better not warm up on stage, Maggie. Randall's there."

"I'll stay in the wings, out of his way."

"Well, don't say I didn't warn you."

I crossed the hall and opened the stage door but didn't enter because Larry Randall blocked my way.

"Out! Out! We're still rehearsing. Nobody's allowed except my own people. Is that crystal clear?"

I backed away, aware of dancers sprawled across the floor of the stage. Were they performing or merely resting? No music accompanied them. Or had he shut off the tape when he heard me coming? All summer he had barred outsiders from his rehearsals. As if anyone would want to steal his dumb ideas! He may be a good dancer, but so far the ballets he has choreographed have been absolutely terrible.

I lifted my chin. "Well, where can I warm up, then?"

"That's hardly my concern. You're in Eriksen's ballet. Ask him. Maybe get him to supervise. Since you have such a hankering for him."

Blushing, fuming, I dashed back to the dressing room. "That Randall!" I cried. I exercised so furiously that one of the girls said, "Slow down, Maggie, before you pull something!"

Gradually the kids in Blikk's ballet wandered in to warm up and make up. Anita and Kathy, careful to choose tables at opposite ends of the room, didn't speak. Armando barged in, peeked over the dividing curtain, and shouted, "*Hola, chicas!*"

A few minutes later Randall's sweating dancers dragged themselves into the dressing room.

"How's it going?" I asked the one who dropped onto

the chair next to mine. She hid her face in the crook of her elbow. "Don't ask."

A knock sounded on our door. "Fifteen minutes."

The call was only for the kids in the first ballet, but my heart started jumping. Would I dance okay when my turn finally did come? I had rehearsed only once in *pointe* shoes and never in Natalie's tunic. I tied myself into it now, a scarlet scrap of nylon. In the studio mirror my reflection looked slender and at the same time very feminine. Would Blikk think so too? Oh, I hoped so! I hugged myself and spun a double *pirouette*.

When the second call came, the kids in the first ballet crowded to the doorway in long white tutus borrowed from our production of *Les Sylphides*. White wisps. They reminded me of Lupe slipping into the fog the afternoon she disappeared from our apartment. A shiver went through me.

Strains of Chopin sang across the corridor now. I hoped my parents had arrived. They would probably enjoy the Chopin ballet more than Blikk's modern rock.

I paced the studio, did *pliés*, paced some more, did *frappés*. Soon muted applause drifted into the room, then came the dancers like a fresh breeze into the stale, cologne-scented air. Excited, laughing, chattering, they discussed the performance and their goofs. "Lord, I'm glad it's over!" one of the girls said.

I sighed. Amen! If only *The Volcanoes* was over too!

The first intermission dragged on forever. Would my parents come backstage? But they knew better than to bother me before I danced.

"Five minutes" came the call for Randall's dancers.

Groans greeted it from both sides of the dressing room curtain.

"Here goes nothing," said one of the dancers.

"Hope we aren't tarred and feathered," another said.

They trooped out, then silence. I tramped up and down the room. Put on more eyeliner. Sprinkled on another layer of baby powder. Still only silence from across the corridor. The silence continued for five, ten, twenty, minutes. I measured its length by the clock on the studio wall.

"What's going on, do you suppose?" I asked, chewing a hangnail.

"Who cares?" Anita said.

"Who asked you?" Kathy said.

"Girls! Girls!" Armando called. He poked his head over the dividing curtain and grinned. "You're all fully clothed, I see. Too bad!"

I opened the door into the corridor and listened.

From the stage came slitherings, thuds, plops, and whacks, but no music. From the audience came snorts, grunts, rustlings, and a regular contagion of coughs. Finally the curtain swished shut. A pattering of applause followed. And boos. Lots of boos. A regular hail of boos.

Shaking my head, I backed into the dressing room. I'd die if they booed Blikk's ballet, especially with me, a nobody, dancing the lead. I mean, I had hardly practiced my role at all! At least not since Natalie took it over. I had to talk to Blikk. Out in the corridor I met the audience flowing from the lower studio. I didn't want my parents to see me, but I just had to find Blikk. Finally, there he was.

"Oh, Blikk, I can't do it. Especially not *en pointe*. It was Natalie's idea to dance it that way. So let her. Oh, please, let her! I'd die if they booed your terrific ballet because of me!"

He cupped a hand under my chin. His eyes shone at me, sending a glow through my whole body. And a melting feeling.

"It is your role, Maggie. You created it. You danced it beautifully yesterday. And you look very lovely in the tunic. So feminine."

"Really? Then you really think I'll do okay?"

"I am sure of it."

A few minutes later I was in the wings with the rest of the cast. From the audience came the clatter and rustling and barks of laughter from people returning to their seats after intermission. I missed the comforting trills and throbs of the orchestra tuning up. But hadn't Blikk said I looked

76

feminine? I was no longer really scared. Just awfully nervous. But I was dancing my own role, the one I had created for Blikk and me.

"Places, please," he called. His hand rested briefly on my shoulder, and his eyes gleamed into mine. "You will be wonderful, Maggie. You *are* wonderful."

Then the music exploded, and the dancers churned while I waited with Paul in the wings. The curtain opened.

"Hey, knock 'em dead, Maggie," Paul whispered, when our cue sounded. He nudged me ahead of him into the glare of the lights. I banged on stage, rapping my *pointe* shoes as if they had taps on heels and toes. The music throbbed inside me. I slithered and shimmied and wagged my shoulders.

The music stopped abruptly. With the other dancers I faced stage left. We stared, drew back, then parted to make a path. Between us in the white circle of a spotlight strutted the bandleader, Armando, in his glimmering, shimmering suit of lights. He leaped lightly to the riser in front of the black silhouette of the band. The music blasted again. To its rapid beat he pranced, paused, spun, then pranced, paused, and spun in the opposite direction. Now a spotlight found me too. I leaned against the riser and yearned toward Armando, who for me was Blikk. Always Blikk.

He reached down a hand and pulled me up beside him. Together we rocked in the overlapping circles of our white spots. Soon the other lights faded until the stage was black except for two bright circles, empty except for the bandleader and me. The music remained loud and raucous, but our movements slowed and softened. I rose *sur les pointes,* then raised one toe to the opposite calf in *fondu.* One of his hands went to my bent knee, the other under my buttocks. I jumped, and with one hand he thrust me high above his head. There I perched until he let me descend against his body. Dropping off the riser, he lifted me down, and, arms around each other, we circled the stage in the blue-white glare of our twin spots.

I gazed into his eyes. Silvery gray. Not black. Our *pas*

de deux turned into a love duet with the rock music bellowing a counterpoint. He lifted and released me, spun me to him and away. Whirling around the stage after him, I floated on my summer wind until finally I melted to the floor beneath him. Moments later he became Armando again and stalked away.

Paul found me on the floor and dragged me into the wings while the other dancers resumed rocking. The curtain closed to applause. Thundering applause and cheers. Not a single boo. Oh, thank heavens. Thank heavens.

Paul hugged me. "Hey, Maggie, you were terrific."

"Thanks. You too. All of you!" I murmured, still dazed, still dazzled by the lights. By everything.

"You know it, *pelirrojita*," Armando said. He yanked me on stage to take curtain calls with the entire cast. Soon Blikk joined us. His eyes shone at me. And in front of everybody he kissed me. A lovely, silky brush on the cheek. Nothing like Doug's blazing kiss in the vestibule echoing with the clang of the brass mailboxes.

Someone pushed a bouquet of red roses into my arms. Cammy. Her narrow, white face beamed at me. A single braid of bright hair dangled down her back.

"Here, Maggie. I wish these were from me."

For a second my heart leaped. Who had sent them? Doug? But he was in Alaska. Blikk, maybe. Hadn't he said I looked very feminine?

"They're from your mom and dad," Cammy said.

Chapter Twelve

"You were marvelous, baby!" Mama said when I came from the dressing room with the roses she and Papa had sent. She hugged me, bouquet and all. Her coppery hair smelled of the lilac perfume she always uses.

"Don't crush those roses, Elizabeth!" my father told her. "They cost me an arm and a leg." Then, pushing aside the bouquet, he pulled me against his huge chest. "You were great, Mags. Whoever would have thought . . . ?" he began, then grinned. "But I hope you're keeping up your typing speed."

"Oh, Father!"

"Just teasing, Mags! Just teasing!"

"Well, maybe," I said. For he had come around late and reluctantly to the idea of my being a dancer.

"How beautiful you look, Maggie," my mother said. "Exactly like a ballerina should! Is the shawl new? I always did love that green silk dress. It's lovely, even shortened to street length."

Mama looked beautiful, too, in a white linen suit. Slim and feminine. That's how I felt. Slim and feminine in my thin green silk. Last year I wore it for Doug. My heart twisted. Well, tonight I was wearing it for Blikk. He wasn't in sight. But Joyce came up and gave me a squeeze. "You were terrific, Mag! Your performance should certainly get you your contract."

I sighed. "That'll be the day!"

"Come on," my father said. "I've made dinner reservations and haven't eaten since breakfast. This ten-thirty dining is for the birds! Would you care to join us?'' he asked Joyce.

"Thanks a lot, but I have to work late tonight."

I raised an eyebrow at her.

"It's true, Mag. The committee that's looking for a permanent director wants me to take notes for them tonight."

"Really? Tell me what happens, okay?"

She shook her head. "Sorry. It's confidential."

We left my parents' car in the parking lot across from Ballet Headquarters, then, like Doug at the beginning of the summer, my father barged ahead to La Fleur Bleu. Of all the restaurants in San Francisco, La Fleur Bleu. Again, like Doug, my father gave me no choice. What if that miserable waiter was working tonight?

We followed the maître d' to a table indoors. San Francisco nights, even in mid-August, are rarely warm enough to dine outside.

I draped my shawl over the back of my chair, then peered at the waiters gliding around the dim room. All were strangers, thank heavens. Our waiter tonight was tall and distant. He could even have been the same one who served Doug and me in June. I hunched my shoulders.

"What'll it be, Mags?" my father asked. "Anything you want. This is a celebration."

I smiled. "You order for me." I didn't say, "Like Blikk did"! I only added, "But, Papa, for dessert I'd like the chocolate mousse. It's wonderful here."

After the busboy had cleared away our dinner plates, the waiter brought it to me.

"Well, this is a first, Mags," my father said. "When did you start eating desserts? Aren't dancers still supposed to be skin and bones? Sylphs?"

I shivered, picturing Lupe fading into the twilight at the end of our street.

"What's wrong, Mags? Did I put my foot in it again?"

I shook my head but glanced away and saw Blikk Eriksen pop up from a nearby table. Like a slice of toast from a toaster. I caught my breath.

He bent to kiss a dark-haired woman. Natalie Harper! So they were friends again! I pressed my lips together. Not that he was alone with her. At the same table sat the business manager of the company, a member of the ballet's Board of Directors, and several people I didn't recognize. And Joyce. So all those people must make up the Search Committee. Was Blikk a member too? Or was the committee interviewing him for the directorship? Oh, I hoped so!

"Who are you staring at, Mags?" my father asked.

"Just—just somebody," I stammered, blushing because that somebody—Blikk Eriksen—approached our table. My heart cartwheeled. I almost upset my cup of coffee.

"Uh, Mama, Father, this is Blikk Eriksen. Blikk, my parents."

Bowing over my mother's hand, Blikk seemed about to kiss it but shook it instead.

"Won't you join us for coffee, Mr. Eriksen?" my mother asked.

I slid my spine down the back of the chair. Dear God, let him. No, don't! I mean, I can hardly say a sensible word to him at any time. Talking to him in front of my parents would be a disaster.

"Thank you, Mrs. Adams, but tonight I am somewhat rushed. I wanted to meet you and Dr. Adams, however. And to ask a favor of you." His eyes shone on me, and my insides wobbled.

"The people underwriting my ballet are giving a party tonight in my honor and requested that I bring along a member of the cast. So, if you have finished dining, Maggie, and your parents will spare you, would you accompany me?"

"Oh, yes!"

I leaped up, shoved back my chair, and grabbed my shawl. Then I noticed my parents' blank faces.

"I mean, if you'll excuse me, Mama and Papa. It was a delicious dinner and nice seeing you and all, but we have finished eating and . . ."

My mother rescued me. "Of course, Maggie, run along."

81

My father frowned. Was he going to say no, as if I were still only fourteen years old? But he just said, "Have a good time, Mags."

On the way out of the restaurant, Blikk pressed a hand against the small of my back. Only to guide me, I know, but his fingers burned clear through my dress. My whole body thrilled, felt beautiful and feminine. His hand cupped my elbow when he helped me into the taxi he had called. I was Cinderella in her golden coach. Blikk, my prince.

I imagined his arm around my waist, could almost feel its strength and heat through the tissuey green silk. But Blikk sat apart, leaving enough cold plastic between us to seat a third passenger.

At the party women flocked to him and soon separated us entirely. I knew nobody and, too shy to start a conversation, wandered among the knots of chattering guests until I came to the refreshment table. There, a man, balding, paunchy, not so young, and very drunk, cornered me and turned into a regular octopus. All hands.

"Look what we have here," he said. "Red hair. Green eyes. Green dress. A regular Christmas present, all for me."

I didn't scream, not in this big, elegant room that glittered with half a dozen chandeliers. I tried to hold on to his fumbling hands. But first one, then the other, escaped to grab at me.

"Oh, please don't!"

His hot, sour breath blew into my face. His mouth groped toward mine, but I turned my face aside so that his wet kiss landed on one ear.

"What's the matter, cuddles? Don't you like to cuddle?" A raucous, smelly chortle.

"No!"

"Well, now, maybe you'd like it more private," he said. Clamping an arm around my waist, he dragged me toward a doorway. I tightened my muscles and resisted.

"Let go!"

That's when Blikk showed up and, although shorter and lighter than the man, freed me.

"Hands off!" Blikk said.

"Aw, cool it, fella. She was hanging around looking lost. How was I supposed to know she was your little sweetie?"

"Such an awful, awful man!" I said, clinging to Blikk. He took me in his arms to comfort me. Only to comfort me, I knew, like he used to comfort his dancers in Europe.

"Poor little Maggie! Even at the best of parties unpleasant things happen. I should never have left you alone. A girl as young as you."

"I'm nineteen. Not that young!" I backed out of his arms. "I mean, I'm not a child, Blikk."

He smiled. "No, only a charming innocent."

"Well, I don't know."

"I know. My former wife was charming but not very innocent."

His mouth tightened. His face went blank. What would it be like to be married to Blikk Eriksen? To eat across the table from him? To watch him shave? To sleep with him? My face grew hot. I just meant to sleep in the same bed with him. Not to make love. For some reason I never really thought about having sex with Blikk Eriksen. Maybe I was still too dazzled. Maybe later. With Doug I used to think about it a lot.

I wet my lips. "I'm—I'm sorry about your wife, Blikk."

"Yes. Well, it is all over now. And so is this party. For us at least, Maggie. It is time to thank our hostess. I will see you safely home."

In the taxi we sat far apart and silent. Was he brooding over his ex-wife? From Blikk's hint she must have been unfaithful. Unfaithful to a wonderful man like Blikk? Maybe he had been away too much, doing ballets all over Europe and America. What a puzzle, why some marriages worked and others didn't. Lupe's to Eddy never had a chance, of course. What about mine if I had married Doug last summer? Tears filled my eyes.

At my apartment I dragged open the door on my side of the cab.

"Wait a minute, Maggie." Blikk leaped out and bounded

83

around the taxi. "In Europe a gentleman always escorts a lady to her door."

"Thanks, but it's only a few feet."

"Nevertheless," he said.

And I was glad he came with me. For inside the vestibule lurked a man. Blikk saw him first. "Salazar? What are you doing here?"

"Eddy!" I exclaimed.

"Yeah!" Eddy said, scowling. "The lock's been changed, so my key doesn't fit anymore. I know Lupe's hid out up there."

I backed against Blikk, grateful to feel his arms come around me.

"You're wrong, Eddy," I said, brave with Blikk so close. "I haven't seen Lupe for ages."

"That's what you say. But I'm going up and find out for myself."

"I suggest you leave, Salazar," Blikk said.

"Not till I check out the apartment."

"Then I will be forced to call the police," Blikk said.

"You'll have to get to a phone first."

Blikk opened the door and yelled at the driver, "Cabbie, please radio for the police."

"Okay! Never mind," Eddy said. "I get the picture. But I'll be back." He shoved his hands into his pockets and shambled off.

"Let me have your keys, Maggie."

Opening the inner vestibule door, he went up the narrow flight of stairs with me and along the dim, second-floor hall. It smelled of cabbage from the White Russians' apartment and of sour red wine from the Italians'.

"It's this one," I said outside my door.

He unlocked it, then handed me my keys. His face in the sallow light from the stairwell bulb seemed leaner and more fine-boned than ever. I wanted to ask him in, but how could I with my roommates maybe gone to bed already or watching TV in their underwear?

"Uh, good night, Blikk. Thanks for a lovely evening."

"The pleasure was mine, Maggie."

As he turned to leave I touched his arm. "Would you—I mean, just to say good night—would you kiss me, Blikk?"

He smiled. "Yes, of course, Maggie."

His hands lightly cupped my shoulders. Shutting my eyes, I tilted up my mouth. His lips touched my forehead, though, barely grazing it with the same kind of tender kiss Papa used to give me when I was his little three-year-old Mags.

Chapter Thirteen

I was still curled up in bed the next morning when, in nothing but a short terry-cloth wrapper, Joyce dropped onto my narrow mattress. She shook *The Chronicle* in my face.

"Look, Mag, you're famous! Read this review."

"Let me see!" I sat up in my nightgown, grabbed the newspaper, and started reading where Joyce's stubby finger pointed.

SUMMER BALLET OFF WITH A BANG, A BOMB, AND A BAUBLE, said the headline.

"Corrrrny!" I said.

Joyce grinned and scooped back one big, round breast that had escaped from her wrapper.

"Sounds as if the headline writer got a little carried away with his alliteration, all right! So did the reviewer."

"But which word describes Blikk's ballet?" I asked, pushing my flood of hair behind my ears.

"For gosh sakes, will you two shut up?" Kathy yelled from her mattress a few feet away. "It's the very crack of dawn!"

"Aren't you interested in the reviews?" Joyce asked.

"I couldn't care less. Just let me sleep!"

"So sleep," I said, and skimmed the column of print.

Joyce laughed. "Quit frowning, Mag. It's okay. The reviewer liked Blikk Eriksen's ballet. Also you."

"Me? Where? Where does it say he liked me?"

"Here," Joyce said, holding the paper close to her face

because, although she had put on her wrapper, she hadn't put in her contacts. She jabbed a finger at a sentence in the middle of the article.

" 'Lithe young apprentice Maggie Adams danced a wistful, wishful star-struck rock fan,' " Joyce read aloud.

I found the place and mouthed the sentence to myself. The words didn't seem to have any connection with me. I frowned at them, at the adjectives the critic had used to describe me. Lithe, young, star-struck, wistful. Also wishful. Was that how people saw me?

"Is that all the review says about me?" I asked. "Doesn't it talk about my *ballon?* Or how I project the character?"

"Heavens, doll, be happy. You're the only dancer mentioned at all. The reviewer spends most of the article lambasting Randall's bomb. Listen to this.

" 'Larry Randall, a fine *danseur noble* whose past efforts at choreography have hardly matched his dancing ability, bombed out entirely last night with a new ballet, *Atomic Atoms.* Dancers were garbed in gray, black, and white sheaths to represent atoms but looked more like gigantic slugs. They slithered around the floor to the accompaniment of rhythmless electronic whines that resembled the recorded whistling of whales. No music. No dancing. No ballet! Period! And if it hadn't been for the plastic floor covering, the entire cast would be spending today tweezing out slivers from arms, legs, shoulders and backsides.' "

Joyce shook her head. "Poor Randall. I'd be sorry for him if he were just halfway human!"

"He's subhuman," I snapped, remembering his slur about my feelings for Blikk. "And what if he becomes permanent director? A real disaster! Was the committee interviewing Blikk for the job last night?"

Joyce sighed. "It was. But it was more or less a token interview. A courtesy to a visiting choreographer. Everybody—except ravishing Natalie Harper, naturally," she put in dryly, "seems to be leaning toward Randall because of his length of time with the company. Even if the critics are forever panning his ballets. Including this one, it turns

87

out. Of course, they didn't like Bob Morris's, either. Called it 'a warmed-over *Les Sylphides*.' ''

Suddenly a smile bloomed on her face. "But they absolutely loved Blikk's ballet!" She sounded ecstatic, even happier than when her own ballets have won honorable mentions in various amateur competitions. In a rich, throaty voice she spouted the review as if it were poetry.

" 'Eriksen's new ballet is lighthearted, brash, rhythmic, and filled with daring, original lifts. But for all its gaiety and freshness, or perhaps because of these very qualities, *The Volcanoes* expresses the poignancy, the tenderness, and, yes, the sadness of youth.' ''

"Wow!" Kathy said, yawning. "And here I thought we were just having fun!"

We continued having fun in Blikk's ballet or expressing the sadness of youth, depending on your point of view, until late in August. But, for me, the real sadness came one afternoon after the last performance. I wouldn't be seeing Blikk for three whole weeks! And it looked as if I wouldn't even get to say good-bye to him properly. At least not very privately, with maybe a quick hug and a good-bye kiss.

When we dragged ourselves into the wings following the final curtain call, he made a short speech to the assembled cast of *The Volcanoes*.

"You all danced wonderfully. Every one of you. In every performance." He stood there all in white, sort of shining. His eyes too.

"You are what give *The Volcanoes* its charm, its success," he continued. "I thank you from the bottom of my heart. Now have wonderful, restful vacations. And when you return in September, I look forward to working with all of you again. Good-bye."

While everybody except me yelled, "Good-bye. Good-bye," he strode toward the door.

Disappointed, sad, I pressed my lips together and tried not to cry. Then, just before Blikk reached the hall, he turned and beckoned to me. Only to me. A thrill spun through me. I bounded to him.

"Yes, Blikk?"

He put his arm around me. "Rest up, Maggie. Have an especially good rest because this fall you will not only be rehearsing the lead in *The Volcanoes*, you will have a very important role, a major role, in *The Nutcracker*."

"Oh, Blikk! Which one?"

He smiled. "Patience, Maggie. That is my secret. You will have to wait until you return to find out."

In the dressing room I slid into my green silk dress. For him. For him alone to admire. But when I returned to the corridor, he had gone.

My parents, who had arrived to drive me home for vacation, said how pretty I looked in the dress, though. So did Joyce.

"Too bad gorgeous Doug's not here in person, doll. He'd be dazzled," she said when my family and I stopped at her desk. "According to the postmark on this card that just arrived," she added, grinning and waving it at me, "he's now in Bellingham, Washington. Looks as if he's working his way back to you."

"Really, Joyce? Does he say that? Give it to me."

I snatched the card out of her hand and scanned the handwriting with its leaping capitals and crescent-slashed *t*'s. I groaned. The usual having-a-wonderful-time-wish-you-were-here nonsense. Nothing about missing me or coming back. Scowling, I hunched my shoulders and stuffed it into my satchel. Why did he keep needling me with these stupid cards?

On the drive home my mind went on rehashing that question until all at once I spotted Lupe. Or thought I did.

We were circling the shady avenue through Golden Gate Park when in the low, pale light of late afternoon a flicker of white darted among the dark ferns and rhododendrons and cypress trees. At first it seemed to be only a skinny little girl in a white dress playing tag or hide-and-seek. But what was that smear of red near her shoulder? Catsup? Blood? Or could it be Raggedy Ann's red yarn wig? The girl tilted her head—sharply, lightly—the way a doe tilts

89

hers when she's startled. Lupe moves like that, used to when she danced.

"That's Lupe," I cried. "I just saw her in the shrubbery."

"Are you sure, Mags?" Papa asked.

"Well, no, not positive."

"We can't stop here," he said. "Not in all this traffic. There's no shoulder. I'll turn off as soon as I can."

At the next intersection he swung around the corner and parked. "All right, go see if you can find her."

I sat where I was on the backseat. What if it wasn't Lupe? Was it some half mad stranger? Even if it was Lupe, she wasn't herself anymore. Or hadn't been at our apartment.

"Get going, Mags, or you'll never find her," my father said.

"Aren't you and Mama coming?"

"We'll be right here," my father said. "You're Lupe's friend, so she'll be more likely to come if you go after her by yourself. I'm sure you'll have no trouble handling her."

Mama nodded. "You can do it."

I wasn't so sure, but I had to go alone. I climbed out of the car, crossed the spongy lawn, and inched in among the trees and shrubs. The cold odor of dampness wrapped me like a—a shroud.

"Lupe!" I called. The wind carried away the thin sound of my voice. The dense foliage swallowed it. "Lupe! Where are you?"

No answer. Only deep silence all around me and the drone and slide of traffic on the avenue through the park.

I peered into the underbrush. Nothing but shivering rhododendrons. Had Lupe brushed them and set them quivering? Or was the icy wind off the bay making them shudder? A chill shook me.

I called again, then backed away, afraid to search farther into the shadows. She probably wasn't there, anyway. Probably never had been. Probably I had imagined the whole thing. I ran to the car.

"I—I guess I was wrong," I told my parents, hoping I was, "or else she's hiding from me."

Chapter Fourteen

At home I tried to forget the eeriness of seeing Lupe in Golden Gate Park. *If* the wisp had been Lupe. I watched television. I set the table for dinner. I even reread the sentences Doug had scrawled.

I got to wondering if he really did wish I were with him. If he actually was working his way back to me. Finally I realized what a dreamer I was and buried his card under the underwear in my top dresser drawer. But I continued to think about him as often as I did about ballet and Blikk.

"Dreaming of Doug?" my father asked one afternoon, coming up suddenly behind the chaise lounge where I was lolling beside the swimming pool as usual.

My face burned. "Doug? Of course not," I lied.

My father laughed. "Is that why you look so darned guilty?"

"I am not looking guilty."

"Pardon me. My mistake. I guess it's sunburn, then. Better watch out or you'll burn to a crisp, Mags. And isn't that a spare tire around your middle?"

I quickly sat up and felt my waist.

My father laughed so hard he practically toppled in the pool. Built last fall especially for lap swimming, it stretches long and narrow along the side of the patio.

"Just kidding, Mags. But it wouldn't kill you to skim a few leaves off the pool just once in a while. It was a mistake putting it so close to this big oak."

I did nothing about the leaves but got up enough energy

to swim laps occasionally. Also once a day I worked out at the *barre* in my room. And I dieted. Back to my yogurt lunches. Mostly, however, I still just lay by the pool and daydreamed.

That's what I was doing one morning when I looked down and noticed that the bare skin between my tiny halter and tinier bikini bottom blushed pink and splotchy. I reached for the sunblock on the deck beside me but stopped with hand in midair. A familiar voice boomed above me. I must have jumped a mile.

"Doug! Good grief! Where did you come from? My gosh, I thought you were in Washington or Alaska or someplace."

"Nope. Here I am. Right in your own backyard, Mag." He touched hand to temple in a quick salute. "Back from a summer of drudgery. Manual labor. Ugh! Your mom's studying in the kitchen but said it was okay for me to come out to greet her gorgeous bathing-beauty daughter."

He grinned. My heart caught at his gleaming smile. This was no daydream now. Doug towered above me in jeans bleached cream-colored, white shirt unbuttoned to the waist, sleeves rolled up to the elbows. The mounds of his mus-cled forearms sent a shiver through me. His curly blond head glowed like the sun beneath the gray-green oak leaves. His blue eyes shone with gold flecks. He hunkered down beside me.

"It's so good to see you, Mag. All of you," he said, eyeing the whole length of me.

Flushing, I reached for my towel to cover up.

"Don't do that," he said, grabbing it away.

"But I'm getting sunburned."

"I know exactly how to remedy that. Just what the doctor ordered. Where's the stuff your dad used to go for?"

"Here. But I'll put it on." I grabbed the tube and hid it under me. Doug pried for it. "No, let go," I said, giggling.

"Move over, Mag." He sat on the edge of the lounge, bumped me with his hip, and made a grab for the sunblock.

"I'm going to smear it over every beautiful, sun-warmed inch of you!"

"You can't have it. You can't have it," I cried. "And not so loud, Doug. Mama's right inside."

"She's way back in the kitchen, Mag, and looks way too deep into the books to worry about what we're up to."

"She's studying for statistics, but she can still hear us," I said, struggling to keep the tube out of his reach. "I'll put it on myself, thank you."

"Oh, yeah?" He dug under me, snatched it, and pinned me, squirming and giggling, to the lounge. "Know what your problem is? You're afraid my hands are cold. But they're as warm as my heart, Mag. So lie still."

After a few not very serious attempts to twist away from him, I did what he asked. I hardly breathed. My daydreams were coming true.

Smiling, humming softly, he unscrewed the cap. When his hand touched my warm skin, a delicious shiver ran through me. I reached my arms around his neck. "Oh, Doug!"

"Mag! I've been dreaming of this."

"Me, too, Doug."

He bent over and kissed and kissed me.

Finally he propped himself up on one elbow. His eyes were so blue, so clear, except for the gleaming flecks of gold. I ran a finger along his jaw where his red beard used to grow. He caught my hand and kissed it.

"We need to talk, honey."

"I suppose." But I kissed the long furrow that ran from his strong throat to his dark little belly button. He hugged me to him, then let go.

"We've got to talk, Mag. Out there in the boonies all I could think about was you. I missed you so much."

"I missed you, too, Doug. Everything about you. Even the flat little tune you're always humming."

"Flat?" he asked, pretending to be indignant. "The music teacher I had in third grade claimed I had perfect pitch!"

"That was third grade," I said, grinning. I pulled his face down and kissed his mouth again and again.

"Mag, we have to talk, remember?"

I sighed. "Okay, if we have to, we have to."

"I was going crazy out there, honey, wondering how you felt. Did you really miss me?"

"Didn't I say so?"

"Yeah, but it sure would have helped if you had let me know."

"Let you know? How could I? There were no return addresses on your silly cards."

"Well, my mother had my address. You could have phoned and asked her for it."

"Oh, sure! Your mother! Are you kidding? She's always hated me. Thought I was interfering with her precious son's education or something. 'Douglas! Douglas!' " I said, mimicking her Swedish accent.

"Don't call me that! I wish my mother wouldn't, either. Teachers called me that at school. I hate it, Mag."

"Okay, but I wasn't about to phone your mother. Especially when I had no idea that you were missing me too. Your cards sure never said so."

"They did too. Every one of them said it. 'I wish you were here. I wish you were here,' I kept writing."

"Don't be silly. All postcards say that. It's something people always write on postcards. A kind of joke. It doesn't mean anything."

"Well, it did with me. I missed you like crazy. That's why I came back. I came back to marry you, honey."

I bounced up. "What?"

He pushed me back down. "Hush up and listen. We drive to Reno tonight. Get a justice of the peace to marry us. Then, in the morning, fly to Boston."

"Boston!" I screamed, so loud that Mom peeked out the living room window. "Quit trying to bully me! I'm not going to Boston. And I'm not giving up something as important to me as ballet!"

"But you can dance back there. Out here I can't get the scholarships I have at MIT. And who knows, I might even

94

wind up having to pay out-of-state tuition to come back to Cal.''

I sighed. No longer angry, just tired. Limp.

"I just can't, Doug. I'm getting leads out here. Two this fall. Oh, don't you see?''

He put his arms around me and drew me against his chest. His heart drummed in my ear.

"I see, honey,'' he said. "I understand. But I have a great idea. A compromise so that we can still get married.''

"How? Just how?''

"We go to Reno, like I said, get married, then in the morning I fly to Boston and you come back here. Dance to your heart's content. Stay on your toes, like the birthday card said,'' he added, grinning, trying to make me laugh, but I wouldn't.

"What would be the sense of being married if we're three thousand miles apart?''

"Lots of people do it, Mag. During wars, for instance. Some people even consider that getting a Ph.D. is kind of like going to war,'' he said, joking.

I didn't laugh.

"Listen, Mag, lots of husbands and wives jet back and forth across the country. We could do that. Spend vacations and holidays together. And it would be for only a few years. Until I get my doctorate. And you're a big-time ballerina, honey,'' he added, grinning.

I shook my head. "It'll take a lot longer than that for me to become a ballerina.''

"I bet it won't. Not with all the talent you must have. Didn't you say you're already starring in two ballets this fall?''

I nodded. "But I'm still only an apprentice. Most choreographers aren't interested in apprentices. Only Blikk.''

He stiffened. "Blikk?''

I bit my lip. I should never have mentioned him. "Well, yes. The two leads I have. They're in ballets he's doing.''

"They would be!''

I flared. "Yes. Because he likes how I dance. You've

never even seen me! Not once! I mean, it's nice to know that someone really appreciates my dancing.''

"I'll bet he appreciates a lot more about you than just your dancing!" Doug growled. "I saw how he ogled you that night in the restaurant. And I understand that you've gone out with him.''

"Once. I went out with him once," I lied, deciding not to mention the party. "Just to lunch. Aren't I allowed to eat?''

Doug's mouth tightened. "Not with Blikk Eriksen, you aren't. You're not to have anything to do with that damned Norwegian. Blikk! Blikk! What is he? One of Santa's reindeer? I don't want him dancing and prancing around my wife.''

Furious, I leaped off the lounge. I clutched my towel in front of me. Talk about Blikk ogling me! Well, I didn't want Doug to. Not anymore.

"There's no danger of my being your wife, Douglas. Not ever. I don't intend to drag around a ball and chain. Or to wear a wedding ring. Not yours, anyway. You're way too jealous. Of me. And of everything I do.''

"Aw, listen, Mag," he said, reaching for me. "I didn't mean—''

"Oh, yes, you did mean! And don't touch me. I'm sick and tired of your jealousy. Sick and tired of listening to the same old garbage. So—so go on back to your precious MIT. See if I care!''

Doug loomed above me.

"All right, Mag. Okay. I'm leaving. And this is it! I won't ask you to marry me again. And I'm not coming back.''

I stood stiff-legged, my body covered with my towel.

"Is that a promise, Doug?''

His blue eyes flamed at me. "Go to blazes!" he muttered, and, ducking his head to avoid a low-hanging oak branch, swung across the patio. He didn't look back, not once, before he disappeared around the corner of the house.

Chapter Fifteen

The minute Doug strode off the patio, I wanted to rush back to San Francisco.

"Baby, baby!" Mama said, catching hold of me as I tore through the kitchen. She wrapped her arms around me. "You have another whole week of vacation. At least wait until tomorrow."

"I can't. I can't stand to be away any longer, Mama. I'll die if I don't get back."

She finally persuaded me to stay overnight, though. The next morning after practically no sleep, I took the train to Third and Townsend, then a bus to Ballet Headquarters. I didn't even stop at the apartment first. I just wanted to see Blikk. I had to see Blikk.

The first person I saw, however, was Joyce Mallory, at the reception desk. Although the company was on vacation, she had to work.

"Back already, Mag? From the suitcase I'd say you just blew into town. What's wrong? You and your dad at it again?"

"You wouldn't believe what happened." And with tears sliding down my face I spilled the whole story. "And he said he'd never be back, Joyce."

She came around her desk and put her arms around me.

"No matter what he said, Mag, he loves you and will be back."

"He won't. And I don't care. Is Blikk here?"

For a minute she didn't answer. "Yes. He's upstairs working on music with a new pianist. Why?"

"I just wondered. I think I'll practice a while. Start getting back in shape. See you."

Although the dressing room hadn't been used for two weeks, the odor of stale sweat hung in the air. The place was bare except for a sleazy gray leotard that hung from its hook upside down like a bat. I hunched my shoulders and, trying not to look at it, changed into a new, fitted green tunic and pale pink tights. I didn't twist my hair into its usual knot. Instead I tied it off my neck with a green silk scarf.

Joyce glanced up when I passed her desk again.

"Looking sharp, Mag. New tunic? Fits you like a glove. Absolutely beautiful! All the studios are free except the one where Blikk is working. That's B, in case you're wondering."

"Thanks." I blushed, annoyed to have her answer a question before I asked it. You can't hide a thing from old Joyce! Not so old, actually. Twenty-two, but she seems older. Maybe because after her parents got divorced and her mother went to work, Joyce took on a lot of responsibility. Besides going to school and taking ballet lessons, she did all the housework and cooking.

Upstairs, I found the double doors to Studio B closed. Through them tinkled the Sugarplum Fairy theme from *The Nutcracker*. Randall was directing it. For once Joyce must be wrong. Randall, not Blikk, was using Studio B.

To make sure, I opened the door a crack. A balding man sat at the piano. And Blikk Eriksen—wonderful Blikk Eriksen in white slacks and a turtleneck shirt—tapped a score on the music stand. Oh, it was so good to see him. He beamed me a welcoming smile.

"Why, Maggie! You have returned early. How nice! Please come in. Is there something I can do for you?"

I clung to the door. If only he would! If only he would take me in his arms. Hold me. Help me forget Doug! Hadn't Blikk said he tries to comfort his dancers, be a father to them? But I wanted him to be a lot more than a father to me!

"Uh, not really. I just came to say hello."

He crossed the studio and peered, frowning, into my face. "You seem upset, Maggie."

His gentleness brought tears to my eyes.

"Uh, not really. I'm—I'm just so glad to be back. So glad to see you again, Blikk."

Smiling, he put an arm around me and led me toward the piano. "You must meet our new pianist, Maggie. He was kind enough to come in this morning to help with some problems I am having with *The Nutcracker*."

"But isn't Larry Randall directing *The Nutcracker?*" I asked, very aware of Blikk's arm around my shoulders. Its light pressure. Its warmth. "What I mean, Blikk, is that the Artistic Director always does."

Blikk smiled. "Not this Artistic Director. Larry Randall finds *The Nutcracker* hackneyed and has passed it along to me."

"Gosh, I'm sorry, Blikk."

"On the contrary, Maggie, I am delighted. I believe that it will not be hackneyed when I finish with it."

"Oh, I'm sure it won't. Can I help you? That's what I really came for. To help you with your choreography. Make notes. Whatever."

He smiled. "Thank you, Maggie. Later, perhaps, I could use you to try out my revisions. See if they are danceable."

"Oh, I'd love to, Blikk."

He slid his arm off my shoulders. "As for helping with the choreography, thank you, no. Too many cooks spoil the broth. And I already have a very able assistant. She has done quite a bit of choreography herself and began assisting me while everybody was away on holiday. She tells me she is your roommate and an old friend. Here she is now."

I caught my breath. Joyce Mallory edged into the room, frowning slightly. She glanced quickly at me. "Hi, Mag," she said, then crossed to the piano.

"I left as soon as Maude arrived to take over, Blikk."

Exchanging smiles, they looked into each other's eyes. They bent over the sheets of music spread on top of the piano. Had they forgotten me? His arm crept around her waist. His hand dropped to her hip and kneaded it in a way that didn't look at all fatherly. Hunching my shoulders, I hurried to the door.

"Are you leaving now, Maggie?" Blikk called, smiling over his shoulder at me.

"I'm—I'm just going next door to practice," I muttered.

"Fine. I will call when I need you."

That'll be the day, I thought. "Sure, Blikk," I said.

I switched on the lights in the neighboring studio. It smelled of damp wood and old, cold sweat. Working at the *barre*, I stretched and concentrated on balance and exact positions. Gradually my muscles warmed and my body moved easily. Every once in a while, though, like a fist to my stomach, came the realization that I had lost Doug. Forever this time. And it looked as if Blikk would much rather comfort my roommate than me.

Finally I wrapped my towel around my shoulders and sneaked past Studio B. From inside came music and laughter. Pressing my lips together, I hurried downstairs and dressed quickly. Ten minutes later I was out of the place and headed for the apartment.

And guess who I found there? Kathy. Also Armando.

Laughing, he tightened his arms around her waist to keep her from bolting off the sofa. The sound of my key in the lock had obviously interrupted something.

"Maggie! You're back early," Kathy said, her face and neck the color of ripe strawberries. "I didn't expect you for at least another week."

Armando only chortled.

"Armando and I, we made up," Kathy added.

"So I see!" I snapped. I mean, I should have been happy for Kathy. I knew how much she longed for Armando. But seeing them together like this, when I already felt left out and lonely, made me feel even more so.

I kicked my suitcase and ballet satchel against the wall

100

and, not looking at Kathy or Armando, went into the kitchen. A mess! Dirty dishes everywhere! Hadn't anyone done them since I left two weeks ago?

Furious, I slammed the kitchen door behind me and ran hot water into the dishpan. Then, with tears spilling off the end of my chin I dashed dishes in and out of the foaming suds. They could all go to blazes! Including Blikk! But mostly Doug!

Chapter Sixteen

Half an hour later while scouring burned-on spaghetti sauce off a frying pan, I heard the front door open and close. Good! Armando must have gone. But he hadn't. The sound was Joyce entering. Watching me closely, she eased herself into the kitchen.

"Sorry about the mess, Mag!"

I shrugged. "Guess you haven't been around much what with the extra help you're giving Blikk Eriksen."

She eyed me. "It's an opportunity I couldn't turn down, Mag. A sort of apprenticeship in choreography. You know how I've always loved it."

"You don't have to explain, Joyce."

She touched my arm. I flicked off her hand and gave her the slimy scouring pad.

"Here. My hands have gotten all crinkly. Besides, it isn't my dirty pan!"

Holding the drippy gray scrap, she looked straight into my eyes. "You'll get Doug back, Mag. If that's what this is all about."

"Sure! Right! 'Marry me and live in Boston!' His non-negotiable demands. Honestly, sometimes I wish Doug were just an easygoing alley cat like Armando Flores!"

"Did somebody mention my name?" Armando asked, swaggering into the kitchen. He pulled a T-shirt over his head, tucked the ends into his jeans, then grabbed me and scratched his bristly chin against my cheek.

"I need my Norelco. Why don't girls ever keep sharp razor blades handy in their bathrooms?"

Joyce snorted. "I presume you've investigated the problem thoroughly and personally."

"Naturally."

He tried to rub his face against hers, too, but she pushed him away.

"Ah, don't be like that, *mujer*. Just because you're moving up to Eriksen."

"None of that, Flores!"

"Only kidding!"

"What's going on?" Kathy asked, coming barefoot into the kitchen. "Any food around? I'm starving." She wrapped her arms around Armando's waist. "Sure is great having you back, lover."

He grinned. "You know it. Come on, we'll go out for breakfast. What do you want? Ham, eggs, or me?"

Joyce groaned. "You're too much, Armando!"

"So what happened to Anita?" I asked Joyce after Kathy and Armando left.

"Anita made the mistake of going home to visit her family. Kathy stayed here and won Armando back. If you can call it winning! And, Mag, I have a message from Blikk. He wonders if you would come to the studio early tomorrow morning to work on *The Nutcracker* with us."

I pushed at my hair. *Us!* Joyce used the pronoun to mean herself and Blikk. It excluded me. I felt excluded again when early the next morning she left the apartment without even waking me. I arrived at the studio a little after nine and found her and Blikk already working.

"Good morning, Maggie—or Mag, as Joyce calls you," Blikk said. "Have you warmed up yet? No? Then please do. By the time you finish, the pianist should have arrived, and we will be ready to have you try out one of our new variations."

I sighed. More exclusive pronouns! *We* and *our*. They included only Joyce and Blikk.

At the *barre* opposite the wall of mirrors I started *pliés*. Since my muscles hurt from yesterday's workout, I exercised slowly and carefully. I tried to concentrate on my turnout and extensions.

But how could I ignore Joyce and Blikk? They leaned against the grand piano so close together that his gray-streaked hair tangled with her short brown bob. They conferred in low voices and made notes in his thick, raggedy notebook. Sometimes he sauntered in little circles, twisting and flapping his hands to indicate strings of ballet steps. Sometimes she bobbed off in small circles of her own, her hands pantomiming a different series of steps.

Between circlings they stood side by side. His lean, wiry body just touched her curves. His arm crept around her waist. His hand slid down to caress her hip. Long looks passed between them.

I chewed my lower lip. How could I ache for Doug and at the same time be jealous of Blikk and Joyce?

When the little bald pianist had scurried in and settled himself at the old grand, Blikk called, "If you are ready for us, Maggie, we are ready for you."

There were those excluding pronouns again! *Us* and *We*.

"Run through it once," Blikk told the pianist, pointing to the place in the score.

The pianist played "The Dance of the Sugarplum Fairy," and in spite of all my troubles a thrill ran through me.

"Gosh, ever since I was four and Mama took me to see *The Nutcracker*, I've wanted to dance Sugarplum."

Joyce laughed. "If it hadn't been for Randall, you would have five years ago," she said, then told the whole story to Blikk.

He smiled. "Poor Maggie! But this time things will be different."

I spun to him. "Am I really finally going to get to dance Sugarplum, then?"

"Slow down, Mag!" Joyce spoke to me but smiled at Blikk. "You won't get to dance Sugarplum, but possibly, just possibly, you'll get to dance the Sugarplum variation. At least Blikk's variation of the Sugarplum variation."

She and Blikk grinned at each other.

104

"Sounds like double talk to me," I said, pouting and feeling left out of their private joke.

"Perhaps," Blikk agreed. His eyes shone at Joyce. "Show Maggie our variation," he told her.

"Our?" I asked, hearing that stupid plural pronoun!

"Yes, Maggie, *our*," he said. "Our combined effort. Mine and Joyce's."

I hunched my shoulders. Like their baby, I thought. The ballet was their baby.

"Not really, Blikk," Joyce said. Another shining look passed between them. "You know I only made a suggestion here and there. But I'll teach you the variation, Mag. It's airy and light and designed especially for you."

"Really?" I asked, wide-eyed, forgetting my jealousy.

"Yes, really! You'll adore it, Mag."

Joyce nodded to the pianist. While he played the Sugarplum music she walked through the floor pattern, named the steps, and gestured them with her hands. I trotted along behind, repeating the gestures and names. Concentrating.

"Got it, Mag?" she asked when the music stopped. "She's a quick study, Blikk. One run-through in my ballets and she'd usually have it."

"Well, this time I want to see the steps again," I said, resenting the quiet intimacy in her voice.

Joyce repeated the combination.

"Now I've got it," I said.

"Then dance it for us, Maggie," Blikk called from beside the piano. "Do not mark. Dance full out."

And I did. Instead of the floor-bound *relevés* and *arabesques* of the old Sugarplum variation, Blikk's version let me skim and spin and flicker my feet. Soon I soared away on my summer wind.

"Wonderful, Maggie," Blikk called.

Joyce hugged me. "Terrific, doll!"

"I love it," I said, "but isn't the Sugarplum Fairy supposed to stay close to the floor, stick to it like a sticky piece of candy?"

"But, Mag, I told you," Joyce said, grinning. "This

105

isn't a variation for the Sugarplum Fairy. She's out of the ballet entirely. We fired her. All her variations go to Clara."

"Really?" I cried, excited. "Then you're getting away from the traditional version the San Francisco Ballet puts on across town. Will a grown-up dancer perform Clara? Like in Baryshnikov's *Nutcracker* and the one the Pacific Northwest Company puts on?"

"That's right, doll!"

"And I'll be dancing Clara? The lead?"

"That's the idea!"

I hugged Joyce, then, rushing to the piano, hugged Blikk too.

"I can't believe it!" I said, tilting my face and laughing. "How wonderful. The only problem is, I won't really get to dance Sugarplum this time, either, will I? But who cares? Who cares?"

I broke away from Joyce and Blikk and spun *piqué* turns around the studio.

Blikk cleared his throat. "Maggie, you must understand that you will dance the lead in only a few performances. At matinees mainly."

"Mag knows that, don't you, doll?" Joyce asked, frowning. Obviously she was afraid I didn't. "Principal dancers will perform Clara most of the time. Including Natalie Harper."

I stopped turning and stared at Blikk and Joyce.

"Natalie will dance Clara? Ten-year-old Clara?"

"She's the prima ballerina, Mag," Joyce said quietly. "She'll dance opening night."

"But how can she pass for a ten-year-old? Gelsey Kirkland did okay in ABT's *Nutcracker* on TV. But Natalie? She's old enough to be Clara's mother."

"Which you certainly are not," Blikk said, grinning at me.

"No," I said. "But I'm no ten-year-old, either. Couldn't you do what they do in movies? Use a kid when the character is little and a grown-up after the character grows up?"

Blikk gazed at me with a frown between his silvery eyes.

"Interesting. What do you think, *elskling?*" he asked, turning to Joyce. She blushed. Joyce blushing? Whatever for? Was it that strange foreign name he had just called her? Something playful in Norwegian? A pet name? A lover's endearment?

Tears stung my eyes. He had never called me anything but Maggie.

Chapter Seventeen

"What was that name Blikk called you this afternoon, Joyce?" I asked while she was cooking supper. "You know, the word that was so guttural and fast. Must have been Norwegian."

She gave a quick stir to the spaghetti. "Just some little joke. You know how he is."

I hunched my shoulders. Yes, I knew. I also knew how his grin and silvery eyes still twisted my heart no matter how much he seemed to like Joyce or how much I missed Doug.

The rest of the week I listened for the Norwegian word but didn't hear it again. Had she asked him not to use it? I forgot about it, though, when classes and rehearsals began, especially after Randall returned from vacation.

Late one afternoon he barged into the studio where Armando and I were working with Joyce and Blikk on their new *pas de deux* for *The Nutcracker*. Randall stood just inside the door, hands planted on his long hips. His eyes, like those of a fish, swiveled up to where I arched in swallow position high atop the pillar of Armando's arm.

"What's going on, Eriksen?"

Blikk tensed but didn't answer right away. He watched us complete the variation. He suggested changes. He told us and the pianist to take a break. Only then did he fold his arms and look at Randall.

"To reply to your question, Mr. Director, we are rehearsing a new second-act *pas de deux*."

"I realize that's what's scheduled," Randall said with his Idaho twang. "But can what I'm seeing be it? Forgive my saying so, Eriksen, but I thought I had bumbled into a carnival act. Some sort of aerial circus. As Acting Artistic Director, I suggest you modify it a bit."

Leaning against the *barre,* I pressed my lips together. To say that about Blikk's lovely lifts! Obnoxious! No wonder Morris had walked out on him!

Blikk smiled, sauntered over to the piano, and studied an open page of his notebook. "I constantly revise, Mr. Director," he said quietly.

"What concerns me most, though, Eriksen, is that you are rehearsing these two." Randall stretched a lanky thumb at Armando and me. "Why not a pair of principals? Why not me and Natalie, for instance?"

With a tight little smile Blikk faced Randall. "But, Mr. Director, as you quite accurately pointed out only minutes ago, the ballet needs changes. I would not want to waste the time of established dancers like you and Miss Harper while I make revisions."

Grunting, Randall raked his fingers through his yellow pompadour. "Cute, Eriksen, cute! Just give me a straight answer. Will these two novices dance leads in actual performances?"

"Only at a few unimportant ones, Mr. Director. Midweek matinees and evenings when principals like you and Miss Harper would prefer not to dance."

Randall's nostrils flared. "But, dammit, there are soloists, even new principals, who'd jump at the chance. Ms. Adams is only an apprentice."

"That could be easily remedied, Mr. Director, by signing her into the company."

Randall rapped his cane against a piano leg. "I'm not here to discuss personnel matters, Eriksen!" he snapped. His eyes rotated to Joyce, who was standing nearby in the curve of the piano. "But since you bring them up, what is she doing here?" He thrust a long, sinewy thumb toward Joyce. "When I saw that blue-haired dame answering the phones downstairs, I assumed the regular receptionist was out sick since it isn't her afternoon off."

Blikk's gaze touched Joyce with a gentleness that made me catch my breath. If only he would look at me like that!

"Miss Mallory assists me," Blikk said. "Maude substitutes for her at my expense."

"Now I've heard everything!" Randall raved. "This time you've gone too far, Eriksen! Joyce Mallory is paid to type and answer phones, not to render services to visiting choreographers. Get back downstairs, Ms. Mallory, if you value your job!"

"One minute, Randall!" Blikk's lean face paled. His jaw tightened. I had never seen him so angry. Not with the impudent waiter. Not with the octopus at the party. "You are interfering with my work as well as bullying my coworker!"

Joyce touched Blikk's arm. "It's all right. I'll go on downstairs. We're nearly finished anyhow."

After she left Blikk eyed Randall. "You and I will have this out privately, Mr. Director. Now, with your permission, I will resume my interrupted rehearsal. Good afternoon!"

Randall stomped out. A few days later, though, he burst into another *Nutcracker* rehearsal and confronted Blikk.

"Eriksen, I'm here again in my capacity as Acting Artistic Director. Natalie tells me some weird story about you using two Claras, a child and an adult, in each performance."

I broke away from the *adagio* Armando and I were practicing and rushed to Blikk. "Really? You're using my idea, Blikk?"

He raised an eyebrow at me, then answered Randall. "Yes, I plan to cast a young student as Clara early in the ballet, an adult dancer later."

Randall's eyes bulged. "Humph! Innovation is one thing, Eriksen, but using two Claras smacks of gimmickry. I had assumed that this farfetched idea came from your receptionist-turned-choreographer. Who, I was delighted to

110

notice, is at her desk this afternoon." Smirking, he pressed his long fingers into a steeple and went on. "But now I hear that this brainstorm is a whim of young Ms. Adams here."

I fled to the *barre* and leaned close to Armando. He gave my waist a friendly squeeze and whispered, "His own ballets could use a few of your whims, *pelirrojita!*"

Randall shifted his weight from one lean hip to the other, angled out his feet, then plowed on.

"A bit of advice, Eriksen, that I've had to learn the hard way. Depend on nobody but yourself. On your own muse, an entity you should not confuse with anyone, male or female, no matter how nubile!" Then, as if shifting gears, Randall turned angry. "So, dammit, man, can't you see how two Claras will confuse people? They'll wonder how the bloody child Clara suddenly becomes the grown-up Clara."

Blikk smoothed his hands together. "I think, Mr. Director, that ballet audiences will grasp the idea. The child and the adult will be costumed in identical white nightgowns. They will have similar body types and hair coloring."

Randall snorted. "I suppose you plan to pair a redheaded brat with Ms. Adams."

"Yes. That should not be difficult. I have noticed one or two little girls with red hair in the corridors."

"Oh, I know one," I blurted from beside Armando. "A little redhead named Cammy Smith. She's in Class Two this fall. I've watched her dance, and she's light and quick and has really good *ballon*. She would be perfect!"

"You see, Mr. Director?" Blikk said, with a lift of the eyebrows and a faint smile, "anything is possible. Even matching up redheads. And may I remind you that my contract allows me complete artistic freedom in the ballets I choreograph for this company!"

Randall jerked his long, handsome profile toward the ceiling. "Keyryst, Eriksen, it'll be a fiasco! I intend to take up this matter with the Board of Directors! Your bizarre casting also. A *corps* dancer and an apprentice in principal roles!"

I shrank against Armando. "Relax, *chiquita*," he said. "We've got Eriksen on our side. He may be little, but he's tough."

After Randall left, Blikk came and put an arm around me. "You are trembling, poor little Maggie! There is no reason to be so upset."

"That's what I told her, boss," Armando said.

"But he'll ruin your ballet, Blikk," I wailed. "He'll take away my leads too. And, dear God, what will happen if Randall becomes permanent Director?"

"Worry about that when it happens, Maggie," Blikk said. "In the meantime, in my ballets you have nothing to fear from Larry Randall."

Maybe not. But I wasn't only in Blikk's ballets. I also had to rehearse productions Randall was directing for the spring season. Not *Atomic Atoms*, thank heavens! By unanimous decision the Board of Directors had forced Randall to drop that dud from the repertoire. He had taken over the restaging of *Giselle* and *Les Sylphides* from Bob Morris, though. And I was in the *corps* of both.

"Hurry, Mag," Joyce whispered when I passed her desk one afternoon on my way upstairs to the first *Les Sylphides* rehearsal. "Randall's in a foul mood. He just found out he's in competition with six other finalists for the directorship. Including Blikk!"

"Blikk!" I squealed, clapping my hands. "How terrific!"

"Maybe," she said, frowning. "Randall has a definite edge, though. Still, he's furious about having any competition at all. So my advice to you, doll, is to be inconspicuous this afternoon! Invisible, if possible!"

I crept into the studio, eased my satchel on the pile near the door, but Randall snapped his head toward me and glared. "The late Ms. Adams!"

I wasn't late. Although Natalie and three other principals were finishing up, the rehearsal for the *corps* dancers wouldn't begin for another fifteen minutes. Half of them dragged in after me. Including Kathy. Barefoot and carrying her *pointe* shoes, she trailed their frayed ribbons behind her. Her bunions blazed an angry red. The infected blister on her right big toe oozed through the bandage. The damaged nail on her left foot had come off, revealing tender, inflamed skin underneath.

Tears shone in her eyes. "I'll never ever be able to get my *pointe* shoes on, let alone dance in them."

Randall must have overheard her. "While you're waiting, young ladies," he called over his shoulder, "put on your *pointe* shoes."

Kathy moaned and whispered, "I just can't!"

"Have you a comment, Ms. Adams?" Randall snapped. Apparently he thought that I was the one whispering. Or pretended to think so.

My face burned. I hunched down, trying to make myself inconspicuous, as Joyce had advised. "Uh, no, Mr. Randall."

"If you're grousing about working on *pointe*, Ms. Adams, let me assure you that even Eriksen, who makes your little adolescent heart go pitty-pat, would insist that you rehearse *sur les pointes*. Which is how we'll do it. Is that crystal clear? So put on your *pointe* shoes. Now!"

Blushing, aware that he was watching me, I crouched forward, pulled on my shoes, and knotted and tucked in the ribbons. Randall turned away, but the mirror reflected his lanky, loose-jointed frame, his flaring nostrils, and his name stamped in gold and in triplicate across the front of his black T-shirt. And to think he'd probably be the permanent Director soon! I shuddered.

Kathy slumped down the wall beside me, a smudged *pointe* shoe in each hand. "What a heel! A real animal," she muttered. "I'm sorry, Maggie. I sprayed on painkiller, but it didn't help a bit. Neither did slitting these crosswise slashes where the shoes press my bunions. Pain. Pain. Pain. What a dilemma! If I put them on, I'll pass out. If I don't, I'll lose my apprenticeship. Not that I really care. Not with my feet hurting so much."

"Of course you care, Kathy," I said. "How about asking Randall to let you wear soft-technique shoes this afternoon?"

She gave a snort, really more of a sob. "Oh, sure! Randall'd fire me on the spot! Come to think of it, that might be better than putting on these stupid *pointe* shoes!"

I pushed at my hair. "I suppose I could try asking him for you," I heard myself saying. I must be crazy!

Her wet eyes pleaded with me. "Oh, Maggie, would you?"

"Well, I guess I could try," I said, then remembered Joyce's warning: *Be invisible, Mag!* But how could I be with my red hair and Randall hating me so much! I might as well try to help Kathy out. What did I have to lose? Only my ballet career, that's all! For which I had already lost Doug!

Sighing, I stood up, balanced first on one toe, then on the other, pretending to test the tips of my new *pointe* shoes. Anything to delay facing Randall. Finally I took a deep breath and edged toward him. I walked on the balls of my feet to prevent the hard tips of my shoes from rapping. I waited until he had finished explaining something to Natalie Harper.

"Uh, excuse me, Mr. Randall," I said, aware of Natalie's faint, twisting smile, of her great liquid eyes shining at me, and of her musky scent that overpowered the room's odor of sweat, rosin, and baby powder. After she turned away he snapped, "Can't you see I'm busy, Ms. Adams?"

"Sorry, Mr. Randall, but I need to talk to you a minute. One of the dancers has an infected blister. She's also lost a toenail. So I was wondering—she was wondering—if maybe you would excuse her from wearing *pointe* shoes this afternoon."

He barked out a laugh and thrust his pelvis forward. "You have all sorts of hidden talents, don't you, Ms. Adams? Assistant choreographer to your heartthrob Eriksen. Now superadvocate for the sore-footed. Which girl has the blister?"

"Kathy. The girl near the door."

"Oh, yes. The well-stacked babe."

My face flamed. I couldn't believe he had said that. He

114

had more to say too. Not just to me, though. No, he lectured the entire cast.

"Ladies and gentlemen, something all of you must learn to accept or quit ballet is the fact that dancers live with pain. I have danced with acute appendicitis, with sprained ankles, with broken feet. So, no matter how many blisters or bunions or lost toenails anybody has, nobody is excused from rehearsing in *pointe* shoes this afternoon! Do I make myself crystal-clear?"

I slumped back to Kathy and dropped down beside her. "Sorry," I whispered.

She sighed. "I didn't really expect he'd say okay, but thanks, Maggie, for trying." She pressed a toe into a shoe and winced. Seeing her pain brought tears to my eyes. Tears of sympathy but also of rage. Hardly knowing what I did, I yanked off my own *pointe* shoes, pulled a pair of soft-leather techniques out of my bag, and put them on.

Kathy stared at me from under pale, wet lashes. "Good grief, what are you doing? He'll fire you, Maggie!"

I gave a little shrug. "He probably will anyway, once he gets the directorship permanently."

"Guess you're right! He's sure to fire me then too. So let him do it now. That'll save wear and tear on my poor feet!" Kathy slipped on her soft techniques too. So did the girl next to her. And the next girl. And the next. I mean, it was like those TV commercials in which rows and rows of standing dominoes topple one after another. Discouraged and a little dazed, I could only watch.

By the time Randall had finished working with the principals, all the *corps* girls were wearing soft-technique shoes. At first he didn't seem to notice.

"Places," he called, rapping his stick. "And if you can't remember the starting position you had in last spring's production, look for the *x*'s I've chalked on the floor."

It was after we had grouped ourselves for the beginning tableau of *Les Sylphides* that he whacked his cane on the floor over and over again.

"*Pointe* shoes are mandatory!" he bellowed, his face turning crimson. "Put them on immediately. Everybody!

Everybody except Maggie Adams. And you, my dear," he said sneering at me, "don't give me that innocent look. I know you're the ringleader. So you're fired. Clear out immediately and stay off the premises."

Chapter Eighteen

"Through already, Mag?" Joyce called when I passed her desk on my way to the dressing room.

"You can say that again!" I mumbled, trying to keep my voice steady.

"Your ankle? You're limping, I see. I'll get an ice pack."

She headed for the refrigerator in the alcove outside the dressing room.

"No! No!" I said, tears starting down my face. "My ankle's okay, but Randall—Randall fired me, Joyce!"

Then, sobbing in her arms, I told her everything.

"Poor Mag! Today was sure not the day to lead a protest movement against Randall! Not that any day is! But he can't just fire you."

"Why not? I'm only an apprentice. He's the boss."

"Well, I'll talk to Blikk as soon as he gets out of his rehearsal."

I backed away from her. I mean, she acted as if she owned Blikk!

"Why shouldn't I talk to Blikk myself?" I asked, lifting my chin. "Besides, what can he do?"

A stillness came over Joyce. "He'll think of something, Mag. He wants you in his ballets, doesn't he?"

"I guess. At least he wants me for something." I bit my lip. That was more than Doug did. I hadn't heard from him since August. Not even a silly postcard.

Joyce led me into the empty dressing room. "Best thing

for you to do right now, Mag, is go home, get some rest, and try to think through your problems with Randall.''

She didn't add, "And your ridiculous feelings for Blikk." But I bet she thought it!

She helped me out of my practice clothes and into jeans and T-shirt. "I'd come with you, but you know how Randall is about my being away from my desk.''

"Oh, I'll be okay," I said, sniffing back tears. "I'll just kill myself, that's all. I mean, no Doug, no ballet.''

"Calm down, Mag," she said quickly, as if afraid I might also add Blikk among my losses. "Don't be so melodramatic, doll! Things'll work out.''

"Oh, sure!" I stuffed damp ballet clothes into my satchel and hoisted its strap over my shoulder. "See you.''

When I walked into our apartment a few minutes later, I hunched my shoulders against the cold. It was so damp that the clothes I had hung up last night still dripped onto the faded, dun-colored carpet. The ancient radiators, one in the living room, another in the bedroom, bubble and hiss a lot but give out almost no heat. You can't turn up the thermostat because it's in the manager's first-floor apartment.

In the kitchen I put water on to boil for tea and lit the oven. I opened its door, pulled over a chair, and huddled in the gassy breath. I had just begun to warm up a little when behind me burst a piercing laugh. I screamed, jumped up, and faced around.

"Lupe!"

She clutched the doorjambs and bobbed between them like a paper skeleton pinned up at Halloween. Dirt streaked her arms, legs, face, and narrow, bare feet. She must have lost the shoes she had been wearing when I last saw her. The dress was the same, though, but dirtier, more faded, in shreds. Her face had shrunk to nothing but bone and smoldering black eyes. A highlight—one single white spark—burned in each black iris. A stale, dead stink enveloped her.

"Maggie's trying to cook herself in the oven," she piped.

A chill shook me. "Lupe, how did you get in? All the locks have been changed."

"Oh, easy, Maggie Paggie. Easy. I buzzed the manager. He remembered me and let me in. I've been hiding in the bedroom till you came home."

She laughed again, a thin, high-pitched shriek. I backed away. If only somebody were here with me! My father. Joyce. Even Kathy. I started toward the phone, but Lupe planted herself between me and it.

"Stay away from the phone, *cariña*." She slurred her old pet name for me, taunted me with it. "I know who you want to call. Eddy."

"No, Lupe. My father."

"Your father, the doctor, to pop crazy Lupe in the hospital? But I'm not crazy, Maggie Paggie. And I'm not going to any hospital."

Behind me, my hands gripped the cold edge of the sink. My voice shook. "Of course not, Lupe. But we've been so worried. Your family too. Wondering where you were."

"In the park, silly."

"Which park?" I asked, frowning. Dear God, was it really Lupe, then, among the rhododendrons last August?

"Why, Golden Gate Park! I heard you calling, 'Lupe! Lupe! Come out where ever you are!' Olly olly oxen free, free, free!'"

I caught my breath. I should have kept looking. "Why didn't you answer, Lupe?"

She giggled. "Because you'd have made us go with you. And we didn't want to. We liked our little tent under the trees, me and Raggedy Ann."

A chill ran through me. The red smear had really been the doll's wig then. "Uh, where's Raggedy Ann now?"

"In the park. She likes it there. The sweet, hot smell of the trees when the sun shines on them. The food too."

I pushed at my hair. "Raggedy Ann likes food?"

Lupe giggled, baring teeth green with scum. Her sour-sweet breath blew in my face. I backed away from the stench. "That's a joke, Maggie Paggie. Are you crazy? Dolls don't eat? Neither do I."

I tried to keep my voice steady. "Don't you eat anything at all, Lupe?"

"Oh, sometimes an orange out of the garbage can. Or a piece of lettuce. But you wouldn't want me to get fat like you, would you, Maggie Paggie?"

Her grin taunted me. Her huge eyes burned at me.

I tried to sound normal. "But, Lupe, the nights are cold now. You need a place to live. A home."

"That's why I came back, silly. The Lord said to."

My chest tightened. "The Lord?"

"Yes. Today in the park where all the people were. He roared over the loudspeaker, 'Lupe, go home to Maggie!' "

I shivered. I couldn't handle this alone. I had to call my father or Joyce or somebody. But Lupe remained planted between me and the phone.

"Uh, I'm making tea, Lupe. Would you like some? Maybe a piece of toast too."

I headed toward the cupboard where we keep the toaster. It's right above the telephone.

"Tricky-wicky!" Lupe said, smirking. "I told you, stay away from that telephone. And I don't want any toast. You weren't listening, Maggie Paggie. I said I don't eat anymore. The Lord says not to!"

I sucked in my breath and glanced toward the phone again.

Lupe wagged a finger at me. "No phone, I said. No! No! No!"

"All right, but I need the teapot to make our tea."

She took it off the counter and handed it to me. Then, as close as my shadow but not touching me, she trailed after me. I brought mugs down from the cupboard and filled them with boiling water. I held the teabag by its tail and dunked it into one mug, then the other. I carried them to the table and slid into the booth.

"Uh, why don't you sit down, too, Lupe?"

Watching me, she backed onto the bench. I cradled my hot mug between my palms, then took a sip of tea. She didn't drink hers. Didn't look at it. Just stared at me. It was awful being alone with her like this. I was scared.

120

Scared for myself. Scared for her. She needed help. And I was the only one who could get it for her. Twice before I had failed, once here in the apartment, once in the park. This time I had to get her to a hospital. Then it came to me. If the Lord talked to her, why couldn't He talk to me?

A swallow of hot tea burned my mouth. "You're—you're not drinking your tea, Lupe. The Lord—uh—the Lord didn't tell you not to drink tea, did He?" I asked.

For the first time she looked at her tea.

"No, silly." Again the laugh. More of a giggle this time. She took a tiny sip. Was she beginning to trust me?

I drew a shaky breath. "But, Lupe, He—the Lord did tell you to come here, didn't He?"

Her glance flew to my face. She frowned, suspicious. "Weren't you listening? I told you He did."

I twisted a wisp of hair around a finger. When Lupe's well, she wouldn't harm anybody, not even with a thoughtless word. But she wasn't well anymore. And she was crafty. What would happen if she found out that I was trying to trick her into the hospital? I chewed my lower lip.

"Well, uh, Lupe, the Lord told me something too. He told me to help you."

Her eyes pinned mine but finally softened. My mind raced ahead. Somehow I had to take her to an emergency room. I didn't dare pick up the phone to call a cab or an ambulance or anything. I had to get her downstairs and into a taxi. A taxi on a San Francisco side street like ours? Impossible! Then I remembered that within walking distance just beyond La Fleur Bleu, a small emergency clinic had recently opened.

I stood up. "Listen, Lupe, the Lord says for you to come with me."

She frowned and rolled her eyes upward as if listening. For the voice of God? I shivered. "I don't hear anything," she said.

"Well, I do," I lied, my chest so tight, it ached. "He's telling me to help you. Do you trust the Lord, Lupe?"

121

She nodded.

"Good." I didn't add, "You've got to trust me too." But I hoped she would.

In the living room, I pulled a sweater off the line and, holding my breath so that I wouldn't smell her, tried to help her put it on.

"Don't touch me!" she yelled. She jerked the sweater out of my hands and thrust her arms into the sleeves. When she had buttoned it, she giggled. "It smells just like you, Maggie Paggie. Johnson's baby powder."

I motioned her out the door, down the stairs, and into the vestibule. There, while passing the brass mailboxes, she drummed them with her open hand. She giggled and I cringed at the deep, metallic clanging, the same echoing reverberations that had followed Doug's kiss.

"Come on, Lupe," I said, shutting my mind to the jangling. "Let's get going."

"Where?" she asked.

"Where the Lord said," I told her, afraid she would bolt if I told her our real destination.

Outside, I crowded her close to the buildings but didn't touch her. We passed The Lost orizons Bar, the ice cream parlor, a deli, several dry cleaning establishments, a movie house, and after a while La Fleur Bleu with all its memories. No time to brood over them now.

A few steps beyond the restaurant gleamed a red cross on the door of a small, glass-fronted shop.

"In here," I told Lupe, trying to hold her with my eyes.

She halted, stiffened. "No! That red cross means it's a hospital."

"It's an emergency clinic, Lupe," I said, realizing it was useless to lie anymore. She knew a hospital when she saw one. But I added, "The Lord told me to bring you here."

She stared at me. I tensed, ready to grab her if she tried to run.

"He really and truly said that?" she asked.

I nodded, believing maybe He had.

She gave a laugh and pushed open the heavy glass door.

Then, dear God, she did something that chilled my heart and brought tears stinging to my eyes. Like mad young Giselle wobbling through steps she had once performed so lightly, Lupe flicked her calves together in a series of quick *brisés* and danced into the clinic.

"Here I am, Lord!"

Chapter Nineteen

The two hours I spent in the emergency clinic with Lupe shook and numbed me. I moved and spoke and did what I had to do as if frozen. As if watching another person.

"We've given her an injection of Haldol," the young doctor told me when he came out to the waiting room. "It's an antipsychotic drug that should quiet her and eventually bring her back to reality. When her brother comes, we'll arrange for her to go to the county hospital in her vicinity."

"But what will happen to her there?" I asked. This was all so new and scary. For Lupe too. What must she be feeling? Or, like me, was she too stunned to feel?

"They'll probably hold her for seventy-two hours. By that time maybe she'll be willing to commit herself for treatment."

"What if she isn't?"

"In that case, if the psychiatrist in charge determines that she is a danger to herself or others, she'll be hospitalized. If not, she'll be released."

"Oh, poor Lupe!"

"Yes, poor Lupe! But we'll keep her safe until her brother comes. You don't need to wait."

"I can't just go off and leave her. May I see her?"

"I'm afraid you won't find it pleasant. She's frightened and angry and very sick. I'm sure that her illness has changed her a great deal. She probably doesn't seem like the person you knew at all. You may go in if you want to, though."

He opened the door into a square white cubicle containing nothing but a cot and a folding metal chair.

"Lupe, here's someone to see you," he said.

Cowering in the corner like a small scared child, she looked at me from under dark, matted lashes. She wasn't sitting on the chair or lying on the cot. With her thin arms wrapped around her knees, she huddled on the floor. Her back wedged into the sharp angle of the room. She glowered at me and shrieked, "You lied! You put me in the hospital! I hate you, Maggie Adams!"

I hunched my shoulders. "I had to, Lupe."

"You see?" the young doctor said. "Why don't you just run along home?"

But, although Lupe remained silent and scowling the whole time, I sat across the cubicle from her until her brother Manuel arrived.

Taller and leaner than I remembered, he entered and shook my hand. I had met him only once before. At Lupe's house the day after she collapsed with anorexia nervosa.

"Thank you for waiting with her," he said. "I'm sorry I was so long in coming. It's more than an hour's drive from where we live in San Jose."

"I'm just sorry about Lupe. Please let me know how she makes out," I said, feeling nothing but relief that I could leave now. All I wanted was to climb into bed and sleep and sleep. The round white clock above the admitting desk said seven o'clock.

Outside, the streets were dark. Or seemed dark. Street lamps glowed above the sidewalk, though. The western sky burned pale green beyond the Golden Gate Bridge. And it was cold. At least, I was cold. I buttoned my sweater, but the breeze rushed straight through the stretched wool. When I reached my apartment building, I realized that I hadn't brought my keys. I pushed the buzzer.

"Yes?" came the hollow question over the intercom. It was Joyce's voice, distorted by lengths of metal tubing.

"I forgot my keys."

"Mag! Where have you been? Get up here."

The buzzer clicked the street door open, and completely exhausted, I trudged up the stairs.

At the top of them Joyce grabbed me and dragged me into our apartment. "Mag, we've been frantic. We were just about to phone your parents."

"So you knew."

"Of course we knew, Mag. As soon as she could, Kathy left Randall's rehearsal and came home. She got really scared when she found the oven turned on, its door open, and you gone. Right away she phoned me."

Kathy threw her arms around me in a rare hug. "We were so worried, Maggie!"

I looked around. The room bulged with my friends. They spilled out of the kitchen and wove among the tights and underwear on the drying line. They eyed me as if I had dropped from Mars. Joyce. Kathy. Paul. Seth. Armando. And from the sofa Blikk smiled at me.

"What really puzzled us, Mag—upset us—were the two mugs of lukewarm tea on the kitchen table," Joyce said. "We couldn't imagine—"

"Mine and Lupe's," I said.

"Lupe's!" everybody exclaimed.

And I realized that they didn't know about Lupe, after all, so I told them.

Joyce held me quietly. Finally she said, "We thought you—uh—disappeared because Randall fired you."

I backed away, sighing. "Disappearing wouldn't help that, would it?"

"No," Joyce said, "but maybe a good night's sleep would, and a little supper. How about a glass of wine and some of the quiche I'm fixing for Blikk and me?"

"For Blikk?" I asked with that familiar prick of jealousy. Ridiculous! I admired Blikk. Was flattered by his attention. And I really, really liked him. Right now his sweet, silvery eyes shimmered at me from the sofa bed. I looked away, finally knowing what his gentle glances had

126

tried to tell me all along: my silly, obvious crush on him had developed only because Doug had up and left me.

Doug's jealousy was ridiculous too. But might not have been, I thought, cringing, if Blikk were like the octopus at the party and not a man of honor.

"What'll it be, Mag?" Joyce asked again. "Quiche or not?"

"Uh, no quiche for me. I'll just make myself a cup of hot chocolate and call it a night."

Seth and Paul had plans and left. So did Armando and Kathy. I mixed hot water with powdered chocolate and carried my cup to the booth. Blikk slid onto the bench across from me.

"I have very little influence with Randall, Maggie," Blikk said, "but tomorrow I will try to talk sense to him."

Nodding, I stared into my cup. My face grew as hot as the steaming, fragrant chocolate. "Thanks," I mumbled. "Thanks a lot. And not just for that, Blikk, but for, well, everything," I added, my face flaming.

His eyes shone at me. "Of course, Maggie. My pleasure."

In the morning I sat in my bathrobe with a mug of warmed-up coffee. Joyce had gone to work. Kathy was still in bed. I peered out the kitchen window at the gray day, which somehow reminded me of Lupe. How awful she must be feeling! Lost and alone and scared. That's how I felt too. Nothing was working out for either of us. Not ballet. Not men. Had giving up dancing to marry Eddy helped bring on her illness? I hunched over my coffee. But Doug hadn't asked that of me. Last August he had even proposed a bi-coastal marriage just so that I could keep on dancing. I sighed. And I hadn't even had time to give him an answer before our quarrel erupted.

I imagined him striding into the kitchen now, ducking his head to avoid the low door frame, saluting me with a quick snap of hand to temple, grabbing me in his arms. My darling Doug! At the very least I owed him an answer.

Jumping up from the table I opened one kitchen drawer

after another. Finally, under a tangle of jar lids, tooth-picks, and rubber bands, I found a pencil stub and a half-used tablet. Turning to a clean page, I wrote, "My darling Doug."

I chewed the eraser and stared while I pondered how to say what I wanted to say. Then, so that I wouldn't change my mind about writing to him, I scribbled as fast as I could.

I've been thinking a lot about us. I've made tons of mistakes, I know that now, but I really do love you, Doug. I can't leave San Francisco, and I realize you have to stay at MIT. But I think we could be really, really happy during the times we are able to be together. So I'm answering Yes, Yes, Yes, if your offer to marry me is still open. I sure hope it is.

> Your loving wife-to-be (I hope),
> Mag

"What are you writing?" Kathy asked from the kitchen doorway.

I slapped the page facedown on the table. "Nothing. Just a shopping list."

Kathy stumbled into the room in a faded nightgown that was ripped out under the arms. Her blond hair spiked out from her head and corkscrewed down her thin neck.

"Any coffee left?" she asked.

"On the stove."

She poured herself a mugful, then dropped onto the bench opposite me. She leaned her elbows on the table and pressed her hands against her white forehead, blue-white where the veins twist just under the skin.

"I might have known it wouldn't last," she said.

"What wouldn't?"

"Me and Armando."

"But you went out with him last night."

"Yeah. And would you believe who came into McDonald's?"

"Anita?"

"Wrong. The great and glamorous Natalie Harpy!"

"So?"

"She was alone. And guess what Armando did? Invited her, a woman old enough to be his mother, to sit at our table."

"Well, I don't much like Natalie, but what's wrong with sharing a table with her? Armando's the friendly type."

"Friendly, all right. He came into McDonald's with me, left with her."

"You mean they just walked out, leaving you sitting there?"

"Might as well have. Oh, Natalie gave me a ride home, but after she dropped me off, she carried him off in her pink Porsche."

"You're kidding!"

"No! Of course, she did mention having trouble with some of the lifts in Blikk's *Nutcracker*. So, of course, bighearted Armando offers to help. 'You don't mind, do you, darling?' she says to me. And off they roar to her apartment to practice. Practice! Right!"

"Maybe they did."

Kathy only snorted. "What time is it, anyway?" she asked.

"Ten-thirty. If you're going to make company class, you'd better get going, Kathy."

"My feet are killing me. I'll walk you over, though."

"But I'm not going. I'm fired, remember?"

She shook her head. "Randall wouldn't even know you were there, Maggie. He's never in class. Takes privately somewhere else these days."

"Well, anyway, I'm not going," I said.

"Me neither."

"And just hand Armando over to Natalie Harper? Sore feet or not, you'd better get to class to protect your interests."

Then, suddenly deciding what I had to do, I added, "I'll come along with you."

"But you said you weren't taking company class."

"I'm not. I have to mail a letter. Then see Randall about my apprenticeship."

Chapter Twenty

Kathy dragged on jeans, sweatshirt, and sandals, but today I wore my green silk with my three-inch heels. I didn't twist my hair into its usual tight knot, either. I let it flow around my shoulders, felt its softness, remembered Doug pressing his face into it, calling it a bright shower of sunlight. I sighed.

"Aren't you ready yet?" Kathy asked.

"In a minute."

I borrowed an envelope from Joyce's top dresser drawer and bent over the kitchen table to address my answer to Doug. I didn't know where he lived in Massachusetts, so under his name I wrote "In care of Mrs. Anderson," and his mother's address in San Jose. I printed PLEASE FORWARD in large letters and hoped she would.

I dropped the letter in a mailbox outside Ballet Headquarters and followed Kathy into the foyer.

Joyce tilted an eyebrow at me when I approached her desk. "Looking great, Mag! What's the occasion?"

"I came to see Randall."

"Mister Randall to you, doll," she said, grinning. "And you're kidding! No? Well, he's in his office. Remember to knock and curtsy. But that sexy dress is wasted on him," she added with her slow half smile.

Shrugging, I crossed the foyer, crossed my fingers, and rapped on the red door.

"Come in," Randall called.

He looked up slowly from behind his desk. First his

130

glance rested on my forehead, then swept gradually down to my feet, where it stuck. I stepped toward his desk, conscious of my heels clicking on the hard floor.

"My, all dolled up for Eriksen?" he asked, smirking. "But you aren't allowed on the premises. You've been fired."

"That's what I've come to talk to you about, Mr. Randall." I spoke slowly to steady my voice. I gripped my hands together at my waist to stop their shaking.

"There's nothing to discuss. You refused to wear *pointe* shoes. Encouraged others not to. Therefore lost your apprenticeship. Period."

"But, Mr. Randall, Kathy's feet were a disaster," I said, forgetting to stay calm. "It would have killed her to go *en pointe*."

"Then perhaps your friend hasn't the stamina to dance professionally," he said, watching the steeple his narrow white hands were shaping. "However, she did go *en pointe* after you left."

"And as a result is limping, is practically crippled this morning," I snapped before I remembered why I had come to see this man.

"You'll be limping, too, if you traipse around on those ankle breakers for very long!" Randall said, eyeing my high heels.

I clenched my fists. My fingernails bit into my palms. But I plunged on with what I had to say.

"Mr. Randall, I graduated from this school at the top of my class. I danced all last year in the *corps*. I took special apprentice classes here besides the company classes. Also I study outside with Jenny Lewis whenever I have time."

He squawked his chair and lengthened the steeple his hands formed. I brushed a friz of hair off my forehead.

"And—and I have principal roles in two of Mr. Eriksen's ballets. I've never been late or missed a class or rehearsal. Is it fair to fire me for one little mistake?"

Silence. His stare rested somewhere between my neck and waist. "If you've gotten all that off your flat chest, Ms. Adams," he said, pleased, I'm sure, to see my face flaming, "I have a few comments to make. Number one, leading a protest movement is no small mistake. Number two, your insolence yesterday was not the only reason I fired you. At your conference last June I made it crystal-clear that a number of complaints had been filed against you."

"But, Mr. Randall . . ." I began. Then seeing his nostrils flare, I shrugged. "Oh, what's the use! Sorry to have wasted your valuable time. And mine."

I marched out. But as soon as the door closed behind me, I sagged against the wall. My face still burned. The worm! The animal! After a moment, though, I crossed to Joyce's desk.

"When does the Board of Directors meet?" I asked.

"He wouldn't listen, I gather," Joyce said. "Third Thursday of the month. That's next week, Mag. The Search Committee is supposed to report on its candidates for Artistic Director that night, so the agenda's pretty crowded. I'll try to get you on, though."

"Thanks. And would you type out a petition for me too?"

"Sure thing, doll. You write it. I'll type it. Here's pencil and paper."

I took them into the dressing room. It was empty except for a mist of sweat and cologne left by dancers who were now upstairs taking class. Where I should be. Longed to be. The piano sang through the building. Feet landing from jumps shook the ceiling. Letting out a long sigh, I sat down and wrote my petition.

"To the members of the Board of Directors: We the undersigned ask that you give Maggie Adams back her apprenticeship. Taking it away seems like harsh punishment for a very minor error in judgment. All Maggie did was wear soft-technique slippers and get others to do the same thing after Mr. Randall refused to excuse an injured dancer from rehearsing in *pointe* shoes last Thursday."

I twisted a lock of hair. The words weren't what my father calls "lawyerese," but they told the facts. Now to end it. I was scribbling "Respectfully yours" when Kathy hobbled into the dressing room. Her nearly white hair straggled to her shoulders. Tears wet her pale, stubby lashes and shone on her cheeks. She dropped onto the bench.

"Your feet again?" I asked.

She nodded. "Everything else too. Including Armando. He's working beside her at the *barre* this very minute. And Anita—Anita says she saw them making out in Natalie's Porsche last night."

"I wouldn't believe a word Anita says," I said.

"But it's true! You should see how he's looking at her up there. And he can't keep his hands off her."

"That's just how Armando is!"

"Well, I've had it with him. With these feet of mine too. And if Randall's going to be the boss around here permanently . . . Anyway, I'm quitting. Going home to Los Angeles where I belong."

"You can't mean it, Kathy!"

"Yes, I can! I'm catching the next Greyhound to L.A." She yanked street clothes on over her tights and leotards.

I frowned. "Will you write, Kathy?"

"Probably not. But I'll think about you sometimes. About you and Doug!"

I grimaced and wondered how long it would take my letter to reach him. If it reached him. If his mother didn't rip it into a hundred thousand pieces.

"Well, this is it," Kathy said. "*Finis*. The end."

In spite of her tears, sore feet, and broken heart, she beamed a smile at me, slung her ballet satchel over her shoulder, and trudged to the door.

"We'll miss you," I said, following her out.

She gave a snort. "Maybe you will, Maggie, but Armando won't. Not Joyce, either, I suspect. Oh, don't look so tragic. Not everybody is cut out to be a dancer. Not me, for instance. My feet, poor things, have been telling me that for a long time. Think on the bright side: I'll never ever have to wear *pointe* shoes again! Hallelujah!"

After she limped out the front door I lay my petition on Joyce's desk.

"Kathy just left," I said.

"So I noticed."

"I mean, for good."

"The kid's had it rough. But maybe she'll meet some nice guy, one totally unlike Armando, settle down in a house with green gables and a white picket fence, and breed a bunch of kids."

I frowned. "Yeah, well, right now that sounds pretty appealing to me too. Anyway, here's the petition. And since I'm not supposed to hang around these sacred premises, would you see if Paul or Armando or somebody could pass it around?"

I left and hurried downtown to take class with Jenny Lewis. I went to her on Saturday too, then all the next week. So, although I was forbidden to take company class, I managed to keep my muscles in shape. Not my nerves, however. They hummed like live electric wires, especially when I was alone in the apartment. Which was most of the time. Joyce was either at work or off somewhere with Blikk. And, of course, Kathy had gone home to L.A. Our three rooms seemed awfully empty without her collapsed in front of the TV, her lumpy feet propped up on the orange-crate coffee table.

I tried to keep busy. I kept the dishes washed. Did laundry until the lines dragged with soggy clothes. I even cleaned the place with a vacuum borrowed from the Italian woman in the next apartment.

Still, every time our phone jangled, my nerves vibrated like the echoing brass mailboxes downstairs. Was it maybe Doug saying that my letter had arrived, that he loved me madly, that he was catching the next plane to San Francisco? It never was.

Was it Joyce calling to tell me that the board had canceled my hearing? She did phone frequently but only to cheer me with news of more and more signatures on the petition. Other friends called to keep up my spirits too.

Not all the calls were about my problems, though. Manuel, Lupe's brother, phoned on Tuesday night.

"Lupe's still in the hospital," he said. "I let her husband know what's happened, but she absolutely refuses to see him."

"I don't blame her," I muttered. "How's she doing?"

"She's getting better. She doesn't hear voices anymore. Although it's too soon to be sure, the doctors think she may have what they call a bipolar disorder. That's a mental illness more commonly known as manic depression. It's supposed to be caused by a chemical imbalance in the brain, which might be triggered by stress. They also think the illness may result from an inherited tendency. She's on lithium, a medication that doctors say sometimes controls the chemical imbalance. Sometimes, doesn't."

After he hung up I phoned my father.

"What Manuel was telling me, Papa, sounds awfully iffy. Will Lupe be okay?"

"It depends on what you mean by okay, Mags. Chances are she'll have the illness all her life, but if the lithium works for her and if she takes it, then she may be able to live fairly normally."

"Poor Lupe."

"Yes, but it tends to be easier to control than other types of mental illnesses. It's a serious problem, though. Speaking of problems, Mags, how is your current one shaping up?"

I took in a sharp breath, thinking that he was talking about Doug.

"Oh, you mean my apprenticeship. I guess I'll know Thursday."

"Well, your mother and I will be thinking about you. We know how much this means to you—I hope the board votes to reinstate you. Of course, if you'd done as I said and kept up your typing speed . . ." he added, chortling.

"Oh, Father!"

I hung up the receiver and stared at the row houses across the street and at the neon sign on a bar at the corner. *Lost orizons. Lost orizons*, flashed the sign. In my mind flashed the words, *Thursday Night. Thursday Night*. And *Doug. Doug.*

Chapter Twenty-one

On Thursday night I couldn't eat the chicken with wine and mushrooms Joyce rushed home to prepare for me and, of course, Blikk. If he wasn't at our apartment these days, she was at his.

"Try a drumstick, Mag," Joyce said. "We don't want you fainting in front of the Board of Directors."

Two hours later I nearly did faint as I followed Joyce and Blikk into the small first-floor studio. Rows of folding chairs lined the room tonight. Among the twelve blue-suited men posted like a jury behind the long table sat the Company's Business Manager and, of course, Larry Randall. For an instant his icy blue stare held my eyes and set me trembling.

Joyce touched my shoulder. "Sit down, Mag. Don't let him intimidate you."

I shook myself. "I—I won't."

"Maggie will be fine," Blikk said. He leaned forward to smile at me across Joyce. "Look at the crowd here to support her."

Jamming the studio were Company members, apprentices, teachers from the ballet school, even quite a few young students with their parents.

"I just hope they're all for me. And not for Randall," I said.

I glanced at a copy of the printed agenda someone had handed me at the door. There it was, my case, as Joyce called it, number nine, at the very end of the list of matters to be taken up by the board. After "Cost of replacing costumes for *Les Sylphides*." After a bid from a new *pointe* shoe supplier. After a report from the Committee for Bringing Ballet to the Public Schools. After a report from the Search Committee for a permanent Director.

"Gosh, I wonder if the Search Committee's reached a decision," I said, frowning.

"I haven't heard a thing," Joyce said. "And I'm sorry you're last tonight, Mag. But it was hard even getting you on the agenda. Your problem didn't arise until so late."

I squeezed her hand. "I know. And thanks. Maybe I'll go get myself a Tab to help pass the time till they get to me."

But at that moment the Chairman of the Board, a small bald man with a huge mustache, cleared his throat and rapped his gavel.

"Judging from the many petitions . . ." he began.

"Many petitions?" I whispered to Joyce. "Does he mean mine? But I only had one."

"The one multiplied, Mag, like rabbits. The miracle of photocopying!"

"Because of the many petitions and letters before me," the chairman was saying, "I assume that the details of this disputed dismissal are already well known to you. Although it appears last on the agenda tonight, we have decided to consider it early so that the many young people here can get home to bed."

I caught my breath, sat up straight, and pushed my frizzing hair behind my ears.

Larry Randall bolted to his feet. "Mr. Chairman, I object. This is not a matter for the board to take up early or late. Even if the—the person involved," he said, sounding as if he wanted to say *defendant*, "even if she were a member of the Company, dismissal is an artistic decision to be made solely at the discretion of the Artistic Director. Besides, she's only an apprentice."

Whistles and boos. The studio rang like a movie house full of kids razzing a villain on a Saturday afternoon.

Somebody—it sounded like Armando—yelled, "Randall's only Acting Director so far, praise the Lord!"

The gavel thudded again.

"Order. Order. Or I'll be forced to clear the room," the chairman said, then turned to Randall. "Larry, I know it's somewhat unusual for the board to take up this matter, but in view of the large number of signatures, we deemed it necessary to hold a hearing at least."

Cheers and shouts of "You can say that again!"

But I slid my spine down the back of the metal folding chair until I was practically sitting on my shoulder blades like Kathy used to. What did the chairman mean by "at least"? Was this a real or a token hearing?

"Pssst, Maggie!" hissed a voice at the back of the room. And up bobbed a small head with bright red hair. Cammy Smith. Her hand wagged frantically. "Hi, Maggie. My mom came too."

The chairman pounded his gavel, and Cammy vanished.

"Young lady, the one with the red hair in the back row. If you wish to speak, young lady, please stand and identify yourself."

Her small hands clinging to the chair in front of her, Cammy eased into view once more. Her round, scared eyes rolled. She leaned to whisper to her mother.

"Well, Mr. Chairman—that's what my mom says to call you—Mr. Chairman, my name's Cammy Smith." She looked at her mother, who nodded and smiled. "Well," Cammy continued in a thin, sweet voice, "I got a bunch of us in the ballet school, students and teachers both, one hundred and thirty-two to be exact, to sign a petition to give Maggie back her apprenticeship."

Cammy glanced at me. I smiled, and her voice grew stronger. "Maggie got fired for helping a friend. That's just not fair. Maggie's the best dancer in the whole entire world. So please give her back her apprenticeship, okay?"

"Yea, Maggie! Yea, Maggie!" called a student. Others joined in. I chewed my lip, but a thrill ran through me.

The gavel came down sharply. "Thank you, Cammy.

Your petition is here before me on the table. You may sit down.''

Cammy dropped from sight like a hand puppet from a stage. Martina stood up.

''Mr. Chairman, I am one of the teachers who signed Cammy's petition to reinstate Maggie Adams's apprentice-ship. Maggie has studied with me since coming to this school five years ago. I consider her hardworking and one of the most outstanding dancers I have taught. My yearly evaluations of her work are on file and will indicate her remarkable progress.''

Cheers and applause. Several people leaped up. Among them Paul and Armando. Armando flapped a hand. ''Mr. Chairman. Mr. Chairman.''

The gavel thundered. ''Order. Order. I recognize the blond man in the center.''

''Thank you, Mr. Chairman. I'm Paul Lawrence. I pre-sented you with a petition signed by one hundred and three people, including Company members, members of the bal-let orchestra, pianists, and staff. We all consider Maggie Adams hardworking, cooperative, and talented. Also a good friend.''

Amid loud clapping, Blikk stood up. ''Mr. Chairman, as one who signed Mr. Lawrence's petition, I wish to speak on Miss Adams's behalf. Although she is still nomi-nally an apprentice, I consider her a principal dancer and have given her and, if her apprenticeship is reinstated, will continue to give her principal roles in the ballets I do for City Ballet.''

''Bravo,'' someone yelled. ''Yea, Maggie!'' called a man.

Joyce nudged me. ''And you were worried!''

I smiled but also shook my head. ''It's really great, but Randall's still the boss. Not to mention being on the board. And just look at the faces of the board members. Not a single smile,'' I added as the shouting continued.

The gavel crashed again and again. ''I must warn all of you once more to conduct yourselves with restraint.'' The chairman waited for quiet, then continued. ''So far tonight

139

the speakers have given only one side of this dispute. To get a more balanced view—''

''Wait a minute, Mr. Chairman,'' Armando interrupted, charging into the aisle. ''I've got something to say! The petition I turned in was signed by a lot of Maggie fans. Members of the Ballet Association, who saw her dance last spring and summer. Balletomanes. Even a couple of real live critics. They think, and so do I, that she got a raw deal and has been getting raw deals ever since she came here because of a certain director's bias against . . .''

Shouts and applause drowned his words. The chairman banged the gavel.

''You are out of order, young man. I must ask you to leave.''

''I thought this was supposed to be a democracy!'' Armando shouted.

I slid down on my chair again. Dear God, now the board would vote against me for sure.

When I dared look up, Armando had gone, but from beside his now vacant seat rose Natalie Harper. Who hated me! I sure knew what she would say!

The people hushed. Slim and straight in a black wool dress, Natalie grasped the back of the chair in front of her. Her great eyes shone at me for a moment, then she turned toward the board. Her harsh voice cut through the silence.

''I'd like to say a word, if you don't mind, Walter, darling,'' she told the chairman. ''I'm not a fan of Maggie Adams. I've often found her flighty, irritating, impulsive, and self-centered. Not to mention capricious and immature.''

The crowd groaned. The gavel hit the table. I hunched down. Was I those things? If so, I'd never get my apprenticeship back!

''However,'' Natalie went on, ''however, I agree that Maggie Adams is a promising dancer, and therefore I signed Armando's petition to have her apprenticeship reinstated. I also have a copy of a letter I should like to read aloud. A letter Robert Morris sent yesterday by express mail to you, Larry darling.''

At the front table Randall stiffened, then sprang up. ''I

140

object, Mr. Chairman. That's a private letter. She has no right . . . How did she get a copy?"

Beside me, Joyce shifted on her chair. Blikk squeezed her hand and smiled into her eyes.

"You didn't?" I whispered to Joyce. "What does it say? How did you manage . . . ?"

"Hush and listen," she said.

"This letter is not at all private, darling," Natalie continued. "It was written to Larry in his capacity as Acting Artistic Director. Do I have your permission to read it, Walter?"

Frowning, I crossed my fingers.

The chairman said, "Very well, Natalie, if you really think it's pertinent to this dispute."

"Oh, very pertinent, darling. The letter begins, 'Dear Larry, last night I received word from a prominent member of CBC that for a very minor infraction you have relieved Maggie Adams of her apprenticeship. First, let me say how astonished I am that she still has an apprenticeship to be relieved of. As you know, I consider Maggie one of City Ballet's most talented dancers. That is why, when I resigned last spring, I left the recommendation that she be given a contract not as a member of the *corps de ballet* but as a Company soloist."

Blikk leaped to his feet amid cries and whistles. "Mr. Chairman! Mr. Chairman! I suggest that instead of restoring Miss Adams's apprenticeship, the board follow the former director's recommendation and give her a contract as a soloist."

Bedlam. The students and many of the adults jumped up cheering. The chairman hammered for order. "I warn you. I warn this audience once again." When people grew quieter, he turned to Randall. "Would you like a chance to speak, Larry?"

I sank back and chewed a lock of hair. Joyce lay a warm hand over my cold one. "Take it easy, doll."

Larry Randall reared out of his chair. His long, pale hands gripped the edge of the table. His mouth twisted into a smile. Or was it a grimace? With Randall it's always hard to tell one from the other.

"It's crystal-clear that Ms. Adams has packed this house with her pals," he droned. "Not that it matters, since our Company is run by this board and not by mob rule. I therefore move, Mr. Chairman, that we clear the room and consider all the board's business including the matter of Ms. Adams's dismissal in executive session."

"Fixed! Fixed!" someone yelled. Others leaped up, shaking their fists.

Tears sprang to my eyes. Executive session meant a session closed to the public. A session in which the board could do anything it pleased. Anything Randall pleased because the other members obviously sided with him. They must be planning to appoint him permanent Director!

The Business Manager seconded Randall's motion, and the board voted unanimously to go into executive session. The chairman rapped the gavel. "Clear the room!"

"How long before you guys decide about Maggie?" Armando called to the board from the doorway.

Blikk laughed. "Your friend Armando has returned, Maggie, and gone right to the heart of the matter."

I bit my lip. "I just hope he doesn't make the chairman mad," I said, seeing the man frown and pull at his beard.

"As long as necessary," he snapped.

"An estimate is all I'm asking for," Armando persisted. "Fifteen minutes? An hour?"

"Young man, this board has a ballet company to run. And, since we no longer have to consider the children in the audience, we will follow the original order of our agenda. So we won't be taking up the matter of Ms. Adams's dismissal until a very late hour. I don't advise you to wait. I don't advise anybody to wait," he added, glancing at me.

I rose, trembling. I mean, now I had lost everything. Doug. My apprenticeship. Probably my whole ballet career! Blikk and Joyce tried to calm me. They led me through the crowded foyer and toward the street.

"No. I want to wait," I said, balking at the door.

"But you heard the chairman, Mag," Joyce said.

"Yes, it will probably be midnight before they come to a decision about your apprenticeship," Blikk said.

"I don't care."

"Well, I care, Mag, and so does Blikk. You look exhausted and need a good night's sleep."

What could I do against the two of them? They walked me home, administered a cup of hot milk, and all but tucked me into bed.

In the morning the phone woke me. It must be late. Pale sunlight slanted into the bedroom. Struggling off my mattress and into the kitchen, I groped for the receiver. It was Joyce calling.

"Get over here, Mag."

"Did they decide, Joyce? Did the board decide yet?"

"Yep! Get over here!" was all she would say.

"Did I—did I get my apprenticeship back?" I asked.

"No, Mag. Sorry."

"Oh." I plopped down on the kitchen floor and let the receiver dangle against the wall.

"Mag! Are you still there?" came Joyce's voice over the swinging receiver.

"Yeah. I guess so."

"Sorry, doll. I couldn't resist teasing you a little. But you're in. You're in. You're being taken into the Company."

I jumped to my feet. "Wow! As Kathy used to say!" Then, without letting go of the receiver so that I was still tethered by the phone cord, I touched my calves together in a *grande cabriole*.

"I was sure they'd side with Randall," I said, gasping for breath. "I wonder how come they didn't?"

"The petitions helped, Mag. Also the letter from Bob Morris."

I frowned, puzzled. "But how did you find out? I mean, the session was closed."

"Blikk told me. Actually, he was the one who decided. About eleven o'clock the board called him back to the meeting. Your appointment was his first decision as our new, permanent Artistic Director."

I started jumping up and down. "Good grief! My gosh! I don't believe it! How wonderful! But how come? I thought Randall was a shoo-in."

"So did I, Mag. So did everybody. But really, Randall had neither the talent for the job nor the support, particularly after the fiasco of his ballet last summer. Not to mention a few other snafus. The letter from Bob Morris was the final straw. And, doll, Blikk instructed me, as his new assistant, to ask you to report to his office immediately to sign a contract as a Company soloist."

Chapter Twenty-two

From apprentice to soloist in one giant step! Like skipping from errand girl to vice-president.

And that wasn't all that made me ecstatic these days. With Blikk's appointment as Artistic Director, the whole atmosphere of City Ballet changed. People laughed more. The air quavered with happiness and hope. It was as if spring had come, although it was December and we were in the middle of the rush and stress of last-minute rehearsals for *The Nutcracker*. Too bad Kathy hadn't waited around for the miraculous change.

Of course, Larry Randall, still *premier danseur*, showed up long-faced for rehearsals, including tonight's dress rehearsal at the downtown theatre.

During a break I sprawled in a red, flounced Spanish costume across two seats in the auditorium. My head rested on the arm of one chair, my knees looped over the next. Ten P.M. Eight hours and only halfway through the second act of *The Nutcracker*. My feet burned. My muscles twitched. When would we finish?

Next to me lounged Joyce with Blikk's thick notebook open on her lap. Beyond her sat Blikk himself.

"You know, Blikk," she said, "we should have Randall run through the lifts with Mag."

I shot up. "What? Tonight? But I'm not dancing Clara at the opening tomorrow. Natalie is. Besides, Armando's always my partner."

Blikk's eyes gleamed at me across Joyce. He grinned.

"Surely it will do no harm, Maggie, to practice briefly with our fine *premier danseur*."

I bit my lip and turned away.

"A good suggestion, *elskling*," Blikk added to Joyce. The strange Norwegian word came out muffled, as if his lips were pressed against her forehead or throat. "*Elskling! Elskling!*" he repeated.

I slumped against the arm of my chair. I mean, part of the spring-in-December aura was their love. They seemed drawn together, their glances, their hands, their bodies. She had bloomed suddenly into beauty, like our neighbor's tulip tree down the peninsula explodes each February into pale magenta blossoms and Mama's primroses ignite into clusters of pink, salmon, and yellow. The air next to me vibrated as if with the bright songs of a mockingbird or the wild, sweet cries of a towee.

Tears filled my eyes. Oh, the bittersweetness. Their happiness. My loneliness. *Doug, please answer my letter. We can be as happy as they are.*

Blikk's voice shook me wide-awake. "Mr. Randall, this time take it with Maggie Adams. On stage, please, Maggie."

I bolted off the seat and crossed the temporary walkway that led from auditorium to stage.

"And, Maggie," Blikk called, "it will not be necessary to change into Clara's costume. Please take off the Spanish costume, though, to give you more freedom of movement."

Corps dancers crowded around me in the wings while I stripped down to the tights and leotard I wore underneath the red satin flounces.

"Wow, Maggie, the *premier danseur!*" they buzzed, smirking, knowing how I hated Randall.

When I edged onto the stage, Natalie Harper, who had been rehearsing with Randall, gave her sloping shoulders a quick shake. "Have fun, darlings! Both of you," she said, and sidled into the wings.

Randall's jaw tightened. His nostrils flared. Crossing my fingers, I inched toward him but avoided looking into his terrible blue eyes. Neither of us spoke. Like the jaws of a shark, his hands clenched my waist. His fingers bit

146

into my flesh. Good grief, his grip would leave purple bruises like tattooed hand prints. If he didn't crush my ribs entirely! But I refused to cry out. I gritted my teeth. We worked through the variation like a pair of robots. Now came the one-armed lifts.

"Relax, Maggie," Blikk called from the auditorium. "You have often done these with Armando. Again please."

I hunched my shoulders and nodded.

Breathless and even more terrified now, I timed my jumps with the upward thrust of Randall's arm, as if to save my very life.

"Better, Maggie," Blikk called. "All right, thank you. And now, Miss Harper, will you resume with Mr. Randall please?"

On opening night I had just pulled on my first-act party costume when Joyce rushed into the *corps* dressing room.

"Mag, Blikk wants to talk to you."

"Now? What's wrong?"

"They just want to talk to you."

"They?"

"Natalie Harper and Blikk. Come on."

Joyce led me upstairs and left me outside Natalie's dressing room. I knocked.

"Please enter, darling," Natalie called.

A regular masquerade party progressed inside. Natalie, in a child's long, old-fashioned nightie, although something slinky would be more suitable for our great ballerina. Blikk, costumed and made up for Drosselmeier, Clara's kind and mysterious godfather. Wild white wig. Tri-cornered hat. Black patch over one eye. Smile gaping where a tooth was blacked out. In Arabian attire, Armando draped an arm around Natalie's waist. A shiny length of scarlet cloth festooned his loins.

He hugged me. "No reason to look so nervous, *pelirrojita*."

"Oh, no? Well, I've got a regular hurricane swirling around in my stomach. You wanted to see me, Blikk?"

He smiled Drosselmeier's slow, gaping grin. "Problems have arisen, Maggie. Natalie will explain."

"Yes, problems, darling. Nothing serious."

She drew Armando to her side again and caressed his silky shoulders. "As you know, darling," she went on to me, "my tendon has bothered me off and on ever since you ran into me last summer."

I frowned. I hadn't run into her, of course. "I'm really sorry," I said.

"You should be!" Then she pouted. "Tonight my poor tendon is aching terribly—mostly, I think, because it suspects that Blikk doesn't appreciate how I dance his new Clara. You don't, do you, darling?"

She fluttered her lashes at Blikk. He only crossed his arms and smiled.

"Besides my sore tendon, that miserable child I'm paired with as Clara chooses tonight of all nights to come down with stomach flu. Of course, I could dance with her understudy, but that little scatterbrain is sure to forget to throw her shoe at the Mouse King or fail to get off or on the stage on cue when we exchange roles."

Natalie gazed into Armando's eyes.

"Most important, my dear friend Armando, who pines to dance the Prince tonight, believes that if you replace me, Maggie, Larry will refuse to perform. In which case, eureka, Armando gets to dance the Prince on opening night."

I gasped. Grinning, Armando grabbed me and, lifting his knees high, polkaed me wildly around the dressing room.

"But we can't!" I cried, pushing him away.

"Why not, *pelirrojita?* It's our big chance. We'll show the critics how terrific we are!"

So that was the strategy. Natalie in a beaded black sheath joined friends out front in a box. I took over her dressing room. I also called my parents to invite them to drive up to see me dance the lead on opening night. The only problem was, Larry Randall didn't cooperate.

"Sorry, Maggie," Blikk said, returning to Natalie's dressing room a little later. "You will have to dance with Larry Randall. Armando miscalculated. We all miscalculated. Randall will not give up performing on opening night, even if," he said, standing in the doorway, "even if it means dancing with a certain redheaded soloist!"

I ran to him. "Then get Natalie back," I pleaded.

"I have already asked her, Maggie," he said, smiling. "Her response was, 'I am no yo-yo, darling. I was ready to dance. Now I am ready not to dance. I am all dressed up and intend to enjoy myself thoroughly!' "

The door closed behind Blikk, and I pulled Clara's lacy white nightgown off its hanger. My icy fingers fumbled with the fastenings. Dear God, my ribs were already sore from Randall's rough handling yesterday. What if he threw me off a *pirouette* tonight? Or dropped me from high above his head?

Little Cammy Smith, called to the theatre to dance the child Clara to my grown-up Clara, was nervous too. And excited.

"Gosh, Maggie," she said minutes before curtain time, "we get to dance on opening night! You and me together!"

I hugged her, then nervously supervised her quick warm-up in the wings.

That's where Randall ambled up on his long, shapely legs.

"So, Ms. Adams, we are to be partners. At last." A thin smile twisted his mouth. A lump of fear welled into my throat. "At least you're not wearing braces anymore!" he added, not seeming to notice, or care, that Cammy was.

"I'd like to kick him!" she whispered after he left. "He's so awful to you, Maggie."

Tears stung my eyes. She reminded me of Lupe. The same fierce loyalty. The same quick tilt of head. The same long white nightgown. Years ago Lupe had danced Clara in just such a gown.

"Places, please," the stage manager called to Cammy, and the others in the first-act party scene. To try to calm myself I did *pliés* and *tendus* in the wings. Blikk and Joyce stood nearby, arms around each other, until his entrance as Drosselmeier.

On stage it was Christmas Eve. Drosselmeier gave Clara

149

a Nutcracker doll. Later a dream. The parlor Christmas tree soared magically. One by one giant mice appeared and killed her brother's tin soldiers. The Mouse King led his mice against her Nutcracker, a Prince now, outnumbered and about to die. Only she could save him. But how? Taking off a slipper, she flung it at the Mouse King and toppled him.

My cue. Unseen by the audience, I crept on stage and traded places with Cammy.

"You were great!" I whispered before she slipped away into the wings.

Confident now and grown-up, I glided to the Prince, who was still wearing his Nutcracker mask. He removed it, and for an instant, Larry Randall peered at me with icy blue eyes. A chill shook me. But I was an adult now. I placed one hand in his and waltzed in his arms.

We circled the stage among *corps de ballet* snowflakes and under a drifting shower of snow slivers. A sleigh skimmed on stage. The Prince and I perched on its gilded seat and glided off, ending Act One.

Hearing the applause, I drew a long, quavering breath. I'd done it. Survived the first act with Randall. Then Joyce, Blikk, Cammy, Armando, everybody clustered to congratulate me. Even Natalie Harper, backstage from her box, drawled, "I've seen worse, darling!"

Only Randall stood apart, eyeing me before he strode off to his dressing room. And I remembered that the worst was still to come. The supported *pirouettes*. The long *pas de deux*. The high one-armed lifts.

In Natalie's dressing room I relined my eyes, brushed out my bushy hair, baby-powdered my shoulders. Pulling out the glittering, many-faceted glass stopper from its vial, I splashed on Natalie's musky perfume. In the lamp-encircled mirror my face peered back at me, pale under the makeup. My eyes stared grass-green and wide-open.

A knock sounded on the door. Dear God, was that my call for the next act already? No, in came Blikk, costumed as Drosselmeier. I ran to him.

"Oh, Blikk, I'm so scared."

"Is it Randall you are afraid of, Maggie?" Blikk asked quietly. "You think that he may try to harm or embarrass you on stage?" Blikk shook his head under its wild white wig. "Not Randall. He knows that hurting you would hurt him more. And already he has lost too much. Now it is time."

Blikk reached for my hand. I drew back. "Isn't that what they say to prisoners about to be executed?"

"Maggie! Maggie! What are we going to do with you?" Smiling, he led me to the wings.

Beyond the curtain, the orchestra sang the lilting *Nutcracker* themes, so familiar, so much a part of my life since I was four and Mama had taken me to see this same ballet. *Corps* dancers, brilliantly costumed, waited on stage to welcome the Prince and the beautiful grown-up Clara. A shadow brushed me. Larry Randall's, cast as he passed between me and the gels in the opposite wings. A chill shook me. I crossed my fingers.

The music swelled. Our music. Our cue. Mine and my Prince's. I placed a cold hand on one of Randall's and, with lifted head, paraded with him through a fountain of soft lights to the dais and the golden throne. To entertain us came Spanish dancers, Arabians, a trio of Russian acrobats, and court ladies.

Now our *pas de deux*. But before rising from our throne, we must look into each other's eyes. Facing the audience, I met his glance and smiled. His back to the audience, he sneered.

"Some ballerina!" he hissed. "A one night stand, though. Eriksen doesn't have a penchant for nymphets the way Morris does. He prefers maturer broads, ones built like his so-called new assistant."

I caught my breath and drew back. Randall's blue eyes pinned me. Ice blue. Glacier blue. Blue glittering with hate. Like the hate in Lupe's eyes the afternoon in the clinic. Alone and scared, how she had hated me! That's how Randall must hate me now.

My lips trembling, I smiled again. Alone and maybe scared, Randall could not, would not, harm me. I extended

151

my hand. Not to Randall but to the lofty blond Prince he had become. My first love. Doug.

Together we glided to center stage where he grasped me in his arms. Not roughly now. Not viciously. No, in front of the audience his hands were gentle. Tender. Our love duet began. *Pirouettes* swept into *attitudes*. *Glissades* into *arabesques*. High lifts into sheer falls.

While he stood back to watch, I danced for him. Little jumps. Shimmering spins. Finally high-soaring leaps that sent me sailing past him, shining with joy, floating on my summer wind.

Now it was his turn to impress me. Endless *pirouettes*. Spectacular air turns. Dazzling, twisting *tours jetés*. Finally in each other's arms again, we skimmed among the circling dancers. Including Drosselmeier with his frightening eye patch and gaping grin. Suddenly I was no longer in my Prince's arms. I was in Drosselmeier's. No. No. I wouldn't give up my dream prince. I pushed Drosselmeier away and searched among the swarming dancers. Gone. Vanished in their midst. And I vanished, too, into the wings, trading places with Cammy again. Back on stage she awoke from our long dream. She was in the parlor. It was Christmas morning.

Applause now. And shouts. *Bravo! Brava!* Hands linked, the dancers formed a line. Cammy took my left hand. Randall ignored my right. He stood apart and bowed alone. Tall. Arrogant. And alone.

The curtain sank and Cammy dashed into the wings. Back she came for the next call, a huge bouquet of red roses clutched to her chest. Among the dark leaves nested an envelope addressed to "My Bride-to-Be."

My heart somersaulted. Flowers from Doug! For his bride-to-be! Had he wired them? No, there he stood in person, towering in the wings. He raised one hand in a jaunty salute. Oh, Doug! Clutching his bouquet, I ran to him. Silently he clasped me in my sweaty white costume, kissed my damp forehead, my oily, lipsticked mouth.

"I got your letter, Mag. Then came instead of phoning. I had to see you. And when I got here tonight, I found out you were dancing. Were the star. A real star. I knew the moment you came on stage. Why didn't you tell me you were so good? So great!"

Clinging to him, I giggled. "I tried, Doug."

"Well, now I know. But I'd already decided to move out here."

"Out here? What about MIT?"

He shrugged. "One school's a lot like another, honey. But there's only one you. My very own ballerina. I have to go back for finals, but let's get married first, okay?"

"Oh, yes!"

Then the stage manager was yelling, "Get out there, Maggie!"

The footlights blazed in my eyes. I hugged Cammy. "He's so wonderful," I whispered as the curtain bounced down. "I love him so much."

"Talking is forbidden on stage!" Larry Randall snapped.

"But, Larry, I'm getting married!"

He grunted. "Not to Eriksen, I presume!"

"Of course not, Larry. To Doug, of course."

Randall snorted and strode off alone.

But when the curtain lifted again and he sauntered back, I repeated an ancient rite between ballerina and *premier danseur*. I handed Larry Randall a single shining rose.

. KAREN STRICKLER DEAN has been a balletomane for more than forty years. She studied with Bronislava and Irina Nijinska in Los Angeles and with the San Francisco Ballet School. In her novels for young readers, she hopes to convey the excitement of ballet while showing a realistic portrait of a dancer's world.

Karen Strickler Dean has been writing since she was nine years old and has written a number of articles and short stories for magazines and educational publications. Presently a school teacher for children with learning disabilities, she lives in Palo Alto, California, with her husband. They have four grown children.